GARO SYNDICATE TRILOGY

ROVENA

Rovena Garo turned the corner of the crowded street into the alley. She knew for sure that she was being followed and there was no way that she was going to lead whoever was trailing her back to her home. This wasn't the first time that she felt as if someone was following her, but that came with the last name that she bore. Being a Garo meant dealing with dangerous situations on a constant basis. She had gotten used to it, really, but that didn't mean that she had to like anything about it.

She tried every door to what she assumed was the back of a warehouse until she finally found one open and ducked into it. Rovena had been taught what to do in circumstances like this. Hell, she had been raised to fight her way out of any situation and she was quite capable, even if her brothers only credited her for being a good shopper.

That was the running family joke and one that she tried to take lightly but hearing them razz her about being a princess or that the only thing she was good at was shopping, hurt her feelings. Not that she'd ever tell them that. Edon was the worst at teasing her and now that Bekim was living in the United States, she didn't hear it from him as much. When he did bother to call her, she'd get an earful about how great his new wife Amra was or how many more weeks it was until she gave birth to their son. Her brothers were all lost in their domestic bliss and that just plain made her sick.

Rovena pulled her gun from her handbag and shoved it back up onto her shoulder. There was no way that she was leaving her favorite Birkin behind, no matter how big and bulky it was. That bag had cost her a small fortune and where she went, it went.

She had almost made her way to the back of the warehouse when she heard the same back door, that she had just used to access the building, open and slam shut. She heard a man's muffled voice fill the air with curses and she stifled her giggle. Rovena loved the thrill of the chase, even if she was the one being chased. Whoever was after her wasn't very good at his job. That was evident from the amount of noise he was making. He had no idea what he was getting himself into by coming for her, but he was about to find out.

Rovena crouched in the corner of the warehouse, which was no easy feat in the heels that she had chosen to wear today. Hell, maybe her brothers were right—maybe she was a princess, but there was no way that she'd let this guy catch her. Princess or not, she'd be the one walking out of that building, and of that, she had no doubt.

Her father used to like to tell her that her overconfidence would be either the end of her or of him. He liked to tease her that she'd most definitely give him a heart attack with the way she lived life with fearless determination, but that was just who he had raised her to be. Her mother died when she was still quite young and being raised by the head of the Garo Syndicate and her three older brothers made her a whole lot tougher than the other girls she knew in town.

"I know that you're in here, sweetheart," the man said. She had guessed that he had given up on being stealthy enough to take her by surprise.

"Come find me asshole," she breathed to herself. Rovena listened as he walked around the side of the warehouse, practically backing her into a corner in the rear of the building. Rovena was essentially trapped and that should scare her to death, but instead, it excited her to no end.

She waited for him to come into view and when she knew that she had a good shot, she took it, nailing him in the upper right thigh. He shouted out in pain and sank to the ground.

"You bitch," the guy spat. He lay on the concrete floor, holding his leg. "I'm going to fucking kill you."

"I'd really like to say that I believe you, but you are the one laying on the ground with a bullet hole in your leg," she taunted. Rovena was careful not to step in the guy's line of fire, not wanting to end up just as bad as he was, or worse. "How about you tell me why you're following me, and I'll call some help for you," she offered.

His laughter filled the warehouse, and she knew that he was trying to egg her on. "You have no idea, do you?" he taunted.

"Why not enlighten me then?" she called back. "You know since I'm so clueless."

"Your brother has pissed off the wrong people, Miss Garo, and if they can't find him, they'll settle for your head on a platter."

"And I'm assuming that you're the one who plans on bringing them my head," she said.

"Sure," he breathed, "and if I fail, there will be others coming for you. You'll never be safe again."

"We'll see about that," she taunted, "but until that happens, I'm going to go on living my life. Sorry that I can't say the same about you." She stepped from the shadows and this time; she didn't aim for his leg. No, this time, she hit him square in the chest and watched as the life drain from his eyes.

"Asshole," she breathed, walking past his dead body and back out into the cold night air.

Rovena pulled her cell phone from her pocket and called her older brother, Edon. He was the head of the Garo family Syndicate now and he'd be the one to help her out of this jam.

"What's up Rovena?" he asked.

"I just killed a man and I need your help," she said.

"What the hell? You killed a man?" he shouted.

"Yeah, he's a Tirana and he followed me into an abandoned warehouse on Fifth Street. He told me that the family wanted their pound of flesh for what Bekim did by taking Amra. They can't find him, so they'll settle for any of us."

"Shit," Edon said. "I knew that this was going to happen.

Bekim went up against the wrong family and now, we're all going to pay the price. Where are you now?" he asked.

"I'm getting a car and I'll be home in about ten minutes," she said.

"You can't go back to your place," he said. "If they've already found you downtown, they'll know where you live. Come to my office," he ordered. "We can figure out where you go from there."

"I have excellent security, Edon," she said. "I'm sure that the Tirana's won't be able to get to me there," she assured.

"It's not safe, Rovena," he growled. "For once, can you please just do what I tell you to do? I'm trying to save your life." That was what he usually said to her when he wanted to boss her around, but this time, he might just be right. The guy in the warehouse warned her that there would be others trying to find her if he failed. Going back to her place might be a huge mistake.

"Fine," she said. "I'll be over to your office in fifteen," she offered. "I'll also consider what you want me to do, but you have to remember that I'm a grown woman now, Edon. The choice will ultimately lie with me, got it?" she asked.

"Whatever—just watch your ass and get here safe," he ordered.

Rovena ended the call and dropped the phone back into her very expensive handbag. "Bossy," she breathed as she waved down a taxi. A promise was a promise though—she'd hear him out and then, she'd have to decide what her next move would be.

JAK

Jak Tirana had to be crazy for agreeing to help Edon Garo's little sister. He was out of his damn mind for saying that he'd take her to America when there was a bounty on her head. She was a princess and the last thing he needed was to have to deal with a Garo princess. In fact, he'd rather do just about anything else than have to deal with her dismissive attitude toward him. What choice did he have? The Tirana's had put a bounty on her head. Hell, the bounty was her head on a silver platter, and he was expected to deliver it to his family. He was in love with Rovena Garo and had been since they were both six years old, but she didn't know that, and probably never would. Rovena had ignored him for the past ten years and he had a feeling that nothing he could do would change that.

"She's not going to go for it, Edon," he said. He had only said that to Rovena's older brother about a dozen times since Edon told him the plan. "She's not going to run off to America with me. You and I both know that she won't run at all. Your sister is a fighter, not a runner."

"I get it, but you're her oldest friend," Edon reminded. He used to be, but that hadn't been true for some time now.

"She hasn't spoken to me in almost ten years now. Edon, she won't listen to me. Hell, she doesn't even listen to you," Jak said.

"Thanks for reminding me of that," Edon grumbled. "Listen, she's my little sister and I can't let her stay in Albania when your family wants her dead," he said.

"Hey, don't blame me for my family's shitty decisions. I'd never hurt your sister, no matter what the bounty is on her head," Jak admitted. "I'm in love with her."

"Jesus," Edon grumbled. "Does she know that?"

"What—no," Jak almost shouted. "And she can't know. I've kept that a secret since we were just kids."

"I'm sorry," Edon said.

"Listen, you and I both know that your sister can be a bit stubborn, and maybe someday I'll work up the nerve to admit my feelings to her, but today is not that day," Jak said. He had a feeling that he might never work up the guts to tell her that he loved her.

"Jak," Edon breathed. "If you love Rovena, help me to save her. Take her to America. Do whatever it takes to make that happen and keep her safe there until I can figure out this mess." Edon looked so sincere, and he knew what his answer had to be. "Please," Edon begged.

"Fine," Jak agreed. "But let me handle this. If you tell her that she has to get on a plane and go with me to America, she'll balk at the idea. We have to come up with a good reason why she needs to head to the States to visit Bekim."

"They are incredibly close. Out of all of us guys, Rovena is closest to Bek," Edon said.

"We can use that to our advantage. Can you get Bekim on the phone? If he asks her to fly to America for a good reason, she'll agree," Jak said.

"Right," Edon said, pulling his cell phone from his jacket pocket. They stood in silence as the phone rang, waiting for Bekim to answer.

"Hello," Bekim said. "Do you have any idea what time it is here?" he grumbled.

Jak knew that it was the middle of the night there, but they needed his help—Rovena's life depended on it.

"Yeah—sorry, brother," Edon said. "Listen, I have Jak Tirana here with me. Our sister is in danger and well, I think she needs to leave Albania for a while."

"In danger how?" Bekim asked, cutting right to the chase.

"The Tirana Syndicate feels that the Garos owe them their pound of flesh for what you did," Jak said.

"And you're going to hurt our little sister to get your revenge?" Bekim shouted.

"No," Jak said. "I'd never hurt your sister. I'm in love with her."

"Jesus, Jak," Edon said. "Can you please stop saying that?"

"So, you and Rovena are together then?" Bekim asked.

"No," Jak admitted. He wished like hell that was the case, but Rovena didn't even give him the time of day usually. "She has no idea how I feel about her, but I want to help. It's why I came straight to Edon when I found out what my family was doing. They sent my cousin after her and well, she ended up killing him, but the next time she might not be so lucky."

"Fuck—she killed a guy?" Bekim asked.

"Yeah, our little sister is tough, but Jak's right. The next time she might not be so lucky. We need to make sure that there's not a next time, Bek. I need you to help us convince her to come to America."

"Why me?" Bekim asked.

"Because she trusts you. You're her favorite, and we all know it. She won't listen to me if I give her the order to leave Albania," Edon admitted.

"And she doesn't even talk to me," Jak said, "so, I'm guessing she won't listen to me either."

"What am I supposed to tell her?" Bekim asked.

"Tell her that you and Amra want her to help with the baby's nursery. She'd never pass up a chance to shop for her new nephew."

"We do need to finish the nursery. The baby will be here in two months," Bekim said. "Are you sure she'll come all the way over here for a shopping spree?" he asked.

"It's like you don't even know our little sister," Edon teased. As if on cue, Rovena walked into Edon's office as if she owned the place. It was one of the things that Jak loved most about her. She was always so self-assured and confident and that turned him completely on.

"Speak of the devil," Edon teased. "I have Bekim on the phone and we were just talking about you."

"Oh," she breathed. God, she was gorgeous, and she didn't even look over at Jak standing in the corner of

Edon's office. She treated him as if he didn't exist and while that should hurt his feelings, it made him want her even more.

"Yeah," Bekim's voice filled the office. "Amra and I were hoping that you'd help us finish designing the nursery."

"Me?" she asked. "She wants me to help design the nursery?"

"Yep," he said. "You know that Amra doesn't have a clue when it comes to decorating and designing. She'd love you to give her a hand. The baby will be here in two months and well, we have nothing ready."

"And this wouldn't have anything to do with the fact that I was chased into a warehouse downtown and forced to kill a man in cold blood. Or the fact that he told me that the Tirana's wouldn't rest until one of us paid them their pound of flesh. Which brings me to my next question," she said, turning to look Jak over. "What the hell is he doing here? You do know that he's a Tirana, right?"

"I know who Jak is," Edon assured. "I also know that I can trust him. If you agree to go visit Bekim and help Amra with the nursery, Jak will accompany you. He'll have inside information and will be able to clue us in if the Tirana's make a move."

"I don't need a babysitter, Edon," she insisted. Jak worried that his being there might have screwed with their plan. Maybe he should have stayed in the shadows and just showed up on the plane just before it took off. That way she wouldn't have had the option to tell him no.

"I need to think about it," she insisted.

"If you think too long, your nephew will be here before his furniture arrives. Plus, it will give you a chance to see our new cabin and explore Colorado a bit. It's really beautiful out here," Bekim said.

Rovena dramatically sighed and hung her head. "Fine," she agreed. "I'll leave in a week or so," she said.

"The jet is fueled and ready to leave tonight," Edon pushed. Jak shot him a look, letting him silently know that he was being a bit too demanding.

"I have to pack," Rovena insisted. "I can't leave tonight."

"Don't pack anything too fancy," Bekim insisted. "You won't need that kind of thing out here."

She stared down Edon and then looked back over at Jak. "I can see that I'm not being given much of a choice in all of this."

"Correct," Edon said.

"Fine, I can be ready to go tonight then. May I have the rest of the afternoon to pack?" she asked. Jak knew that her going back to her place to pack was taking a major chance.

"I'll tag along with her, if that helps," Jak offered. Edon nodded and Rovena threw her hands in the air and let them drop back to her side.

"You are just as bossy as they are," she said to Jak.

"I just want to help keep you safe, Rovena," he said. "Nothing more."

"Mmm," she hummed, and he wondered what that was about. "Let's go then," she ordered. "We'll see you tomorrow, Bekim." Rovena kissed Edon's cheek on the way out of his office and he told her to behave and to be careful.

"Thanks for doing this, Jak," Edon said, holding out his hand to him.

"Anytime," Jak said. He meant it too. He'd do anything to keep her safe, whenever Rovena needed him. He just hoped like hell that she finally noticed him because having her ignore his existence for the past ten years was starting to make him feel that they might not be friends anymore—and that was something that he couldn't live with.

He drove Rovena over to her place, reporting back to his family that she had gone underground. That would at least buy them some time to pack up a few things for her and get to the private jet that Edon had arranged for them. Of course, his uncle wanted to know how he'd gotten his information about Rovena. He lied and told his uncle that he had a trusted source inside the Garo family that gave him the report. Actually, it wasn't too far from the truth. He trusted Edon, even if his family would think him a fool for doing so.

When their two families were at peace, no one even noticed that he hung out with the Garo kids. Edon, Bekim, and Rovena were his closest friends. Then one day, war broke out between the two families—not his war, but he still had to pay the price and let go of his past ties to friends he still missed. When he found out that the Tirana Syndicate was going after Rovena, he had a decision to make—deliver the woman he was still madly in love with or help her to get out of the country before his family sent someone else to do the job in his stead.

"I'd really love to stop for a coffee if we have time before the flight," Rovena said.

"That's not what this is, princess," he breathed. He'd never dare call her that when they were friends. She used to beat up boys who called her a princess back in the day. But there was something about Rovena's coldness toward him that had him wanting to shield his heart when she was around. Using a nickname that she hated would keep her at an arm's distance and that was just what he needed to do while they took their little trip.

"Don't call me that," she spat, "you know I hate it when people call me that, Jak." He knew everything about her—everything, but he wouldn't admit to that now.

"My job is to get you out of the country, princess, not to care about what you like to be called. If you'd rather, I can do the job I'm being paid to do and deliver your head on a platter to my uncle. I'll be sure to send the rest of you back to Edon with my apologies."

Her gasp filled the car, "You wouldn't," she insisted, "you're one of my oldest friends, Jak. You wouldn't hurt me." Playing the friend card wasn't going to work on him—not after all this time.

"That's complete bullshit," Jak growled, "you haven't spoken to me in almost ten years, princess. Hell, as far as you know, I could have been long dead, and you wouldn't have blinked an eye. We used to be friends, but that was a long time ago, Rovena," he said.

"I knew that you weren't dead if that helps," she said, "but our families have been at war, and being your friend wasn't an option for me."

"Again, I'm calling bullshit, princess. You had a choice; you just made the one that shut me out of your life. Just like today, I made a choice to save your life and walk away from my family. I might not ever be able to go back, and I've accepted that because it's for you, Rovena. I wouldn't be able to hurt you or worse, deliver you to my family. I wonder if you'd be able to say the same."

"Don't be so dramatic," she insisted. "I wouldn't hurt you either, Jak. Well, unless you gave me a reason to."

"Yeah, I saw the aftermath of what you did to my cousin. You're still a pretty good shot." She had nailed him in the kneecap, taking him down, and then, she point blank shot him in the chest, murdering him in cold blood. That's when his uncle went ballistic and ordered her head to be brought to him. She murdered his oldest son, and that would never be forgiven. Rovena's only way out would be to leave the country, and still, she'd constantly be looking over her shoulder. His uncle would never give up searching for her.

"I'm sorry that he was your cousin," she whispered, "but, I had no choice. He was coming after me, hunting me down, and he would have done the same to me if I had given him the chance. I just beat him to the punch."

"He was under orders to bring you in," Jak said. "My uncle wanted to sell you off at auction to send Edon a clear message."

"Yeah and selling me off as a sex slave would have been so much better than death," she said. "Either way, I'm not sorry that asshole's dead. I was going to let him live after I shot him in the knee, but he told me that he'd find me and end me. I don't take threats lightly," she said. "If I let him live, I'd have him on my ass too. I eliminated a threat, and now, I have one less Tirana coming for me."

"Two less," Jak whispered. "I'm not coming for you either, Rovena. I want to help you."

"Why would you do that, Jak?" she asked. "As you have

already pointed out, I've ignored you for the past ten years. Why help me and put yourself at risk?" she asked.

"You know why, Rovena," he said, "don't pretend that you don't. My feelings for you haven't changed in the past ten years."

"I see," she whispered. Rovena sat quietly in the seat next to him as he pulled into her place.

"Stay put," he ordered. "There's a gun in the glove box. I won't ask if you know how to use it. I'm going to run in and check everything out. If someone's here, I'll try to get rid of them, but if I can't, you take my car and get to the jet that Edon has waiting at his personal hangar. Got it?" he asked.

"Yes," she breathed. "And Jak," she whispered.

"Yeah?" he asked, turning back to her.

"Be careful," she ordered.

ROVENA

Rovena knew exactly why Jak was helping her. He didn't have to spell it out for her. Ten years ago, just before the war broke out between their two families, he told her that he was in love with her. She told him that he was being an idiot, but that was only because hearing him say those words out loud to her scared the hell out of her. They were just babies back then—only fifteen years old. She had no clue what love was when she was a teenager. All she wanted to do was to have some fun and hang out with her friends.

Her mother was gone, and she was stuck with two older brothers and an overbearing father who liked to control every aspect of their lives. She was out of control—sneaking out of the house, going to parties, spending way too much money, and finding trouble wherever she could. And the whole time, Jak was by her side. He always had her back and she considered him her best friend, but that all changed once he said those words out loud to her. Three simple little words had turned her whole world upside down.

It wasn't too long after Jak admitted that he loved her, that their families started fighting. It was easier for her to blame avoiding Jak on the pending war between their families, but that had nothing to do with her keeping her distance from him. She was fighting her own feelings and not speaking to him made it so much easier to pretend that he didn't exist. Rovena didn't want to end up like her mother—trapped in a marriage where she played the dutiful wife, raising kids, and never having anything for herself. She didn't plan on ever settling down, much to her father's horror, but seeing Jak again had her rethinking all the dreams that she gave up so long ago.

Rovena watched as Jak ran up to her condo building, checking every entrance in and out of her place and when he came back to the SUV where he left her to wait, she almost felt relieved. It only pissed her off that she felt anything toward the man she was supposed to be ignoring. He was a means to an end—he'd get her out of the country and safely to Bekim, and then, he'd be lost to her forever. That worked for her since she was used to not having him in her life at all anymore. He could walk away and leave her, just as she had done to him ten years ago, and that would serve her right.

"All clear?" she asked.

"Yep," he said, "your place is trashed, but whoever was here is gone now. Let's pack some of your stuff and get out of here in case they're watching this place. In and out in ten minutes, got it?" he asked.

"You're bossier than I remember," she assessed. "I can pack in ten minutes, although I'm not happy about my place being trashed."

"I'm sure that Edon will have everything packed up and sent to you, once you're settled in the States," he offered. "In the meantime, just try to look past the mess. We're not here to clean up. We're here to pack necessities."

"Right," she agreed. He helped her out of the SUV, and they made a run for her place, which was no easy feat since she was wearing her highest heels.

"Maybe you should consider running shoes for the trip," he said. Rovena shot him a look and he shrugged, "It was just a suggestion. Those have to be killing your feet."

"I'm used to my heels," she said. "In fact, I consider them all a necessity."

"No," he breathed, opening her already unlocked front door. They had really done a number on it, trying to pry it open. She gasped when she peaked inside at the destruction that they had left behind.

"Heels are not a necessity," he said, "clothing is."

"Heels are clothing," she breathed. Rovena waded through the debris and broken furniture that the Tirana's had left behind, wishing she could have just five minutes alone with the guys who did this to her place.

"You okay?" Jak asked.

"No," she whispered, "I'm pissed off and want to murder whoever did this to my condo, but we're also on a schedule," she said.

He chuckled, "Thank God for schedules. Grab your stuff, honey," he ordered. "You have about eight minutes left. I'll keep watch."

Rovena hurried back to her bedroom, trying to figure out where to even start. Her clothes and shoes were everywhere. Luckily, her suitcase was in her closet still and she pulled it out and opened it, tossing handfuls of clothes in from the floor, quickly filling it. She had no idea what she was packing, but if she got to her brother's house in Colorado and had only evening gowns to wear, it wouldn't be her fault.

Rovena found her second suitcase which someone had tossed across her room, lying against the wall. She opened it and started finding shoes that matched, tossing them into the suitcase. She tried to pack practically, mostly boots, but all were still high heels. She was going to have to do some shopping once she got settled, that was for sure.

"You're taking an entire suitcase of just shoes?" he asked.

"Boots," she corrected.

"Honey, you should pack some sweaters and a coat. I hear Colorado is cold," he said. She hated hearing him call her, "Honey". That should mean something, but it didn't mean a thing between the two of them.

"Don't call me that either," she insisted.

"Call you what?" he asked.

"Honey," she said. "I'm not your honey."

"Not for lack of trying," he mumbled. "Just finish up," he ordered. "You have two minutes."

"Fine," she spat. Rovena grabbed her coat from the back of her closet where it was still hanging and pulled a few sweaters from the top shelf of her closet, tossing them in with her boots. She closed her suitcases and Jak grabbed them from her bed. She picked up four of her precious handbags, refusing to leave them behind, and her mother's jewelry box, where she kept most of her things. She peeked inside, making sure that they were still in there, and breathed a sigh of relief when she found her mother's ring still in the box.

"Good?" Jak asked.

"Yes," she said, "they didn't take my mother's jewelry."

"That's because they weren't here for stuff like that. They were here to kill you and we need to get out of here before they return to do just that," Jak insisted.

"I'm ready," she agreed. Rovena followed Jak out of her condo, taking one last look inside before pulling her door shut behind herself. She was sad to be leaving the place that she had come to love, but if she stayed, the Tirana family would find her and this time, they'd do more than just break her furniture and toss her belongings onto the floor. This time, they'd kill her and bring her head to Jak's uncle. That much was clear, and she wasn't willing to stick around and take the chance that they'd be back to finish the job.

The jet was waiting for them at the hangar, just as Edon promised. She was hoping that she'd be able to see her brother, one more time before she had to leave, but he wasn't there. "Edon's not here," she whispered to herself.

"No, he didn't want to take the chance that he's being watched and would lead the Tirana's right to you. I've been given very specific instructions about what to do and Edon will be in touch when it's safe. Do you trust me, Rovena?" he asked, holding his hand out to her. That was the question of the day. Did she trust a member of the Tirana family? Jak had never done anything to hurt her, but his last name was still Tirana.

She reached for his hand and took it, letting him help her out of the SUV. "I trust you," she said, "for now."

"Gee," he breathed, pulling her up against his body, "Thanks for that."

"Not a problem," she whispered. He smelled so good. It had been ten years since he snuck a kiss and gave her those three little words, but she could still taste him when she closed her eyes and remembered that night. It was etched in her mind—something that would never leave her yet having him so close now brought up a whole slew of new longings that she hadn't expected.

"We should go," he said, releasing her.

"Yes, we wouldn't want our plane taking off without us, would we?" she teased. She grabbed her beloved handbags and heavy coat as Jak grabbed her two big suitcases, lugging them onto the plane for her.

"You pack heavy," he breathed, tossing her suitcases to the side after getting them up the steps to the main cabin.

"You told me to pack necessities and all of those things are necessary," she insisted.

"Because what would you do without fifteen pairs of high-heeled boots in Colorado?" he asked.

"I wouldn't want to find out," she said. "Listen if this is going to be how you handle things—berating me for my necessities, then you don't have to make the trip with me. I'm sure that I'm in very capable hands from here on out," she insisted.

"Okay," he said, and for a minute, she thought that he was going to get off the plane. Instead, he poured himself a drink from the fully stocked bar and sat down in one of the leather chairs. "Let's say I take off and stay here in Albania," he offered. "You go on to America and my uncle sends men after you. How will you avoid them dragging you back here, or worse?" he asked.

"I'd do to them what I did to your cousin," she insisted.

"Sure, and in America, your brother won't be there to bail you out. Edon will have no pull with the police in the States. You'll rot in a jail cell until my uncle pays off another prisoner to kill you in your cell while you're sleeping. If I keep reporting back to him, telling him that I'm on your trail, and his men catch up with us, I can lie and tell them that I got to you before they did. Then, I can find a way to get you back out of trouble."

"I don't need help staying out of trouble, Jak," she insisted.

"Honey, your middle name is trouble," he teased.

"I thought that we already talked about you not calling me honey," she reminded.

"You talked about it, but I never agreed to anything, princess," he said. She rolled her eyes and poured herself a whiskey, neat, sitting across from him on the plane.

"Fine, come with me, if that's what you want to do, but I gave you an out," she said, sipping her drink. He was right, but she'd never admit that to him. If the Tirana's caught up with her in America, she'd have no one to bail her out. Bekim was in Colorado, but she knew that he had no political pool in the US. She'd be stuck and that wouldn't end well for her.

"See princess, I knew you'd see things my way, once you thought about it," Jak taunted. She stuck her tongue out at him, just like she used to do when they were little kids, and he chuckled.

"Jerk," she said, calling him what she used to call him in grade school.

"Brat," he returned, remembering what he used to call her when they were younger. She had missed Jak, not that she'd ever tell him that. He was her best friend and right now, she could use one of them more than anything else.

JAK

They flew overnight and when they landed in New York City, Jak wasn't sure if he was relieved or even more worried that he was going to have to navigate a strange land to find their way across America to where her brother, Bekim was waiting for them.

Bekim's wife was pregnant with their first baby and there was no way that he'd leave her alone back at home to come to claim his little sister. In fact, Rovena promised to murder him if he even thought about doing that. She insisted that she'd be able to find her way out to Colorado, even though she had only been to the States just a few times before. She usually stayed in New York, from what Rovena told him, but this wasn't one of her famous shopping trips. He was sure that the shopping experience out in Colorado was going to prove to be quite boring, from what she was used to.

As soon as they landed, he called back to Albania to let

Edon know that they had made it safely through the first leg of their trip. Her brother told him that he'd gotten word that a jet took off from the Tirana airstrip and he believed that they were trailing Jak and Rovena. That was the very last thing that the two of them needed. He wouldn't be able to deliver her to Bekim if they had a tail. Neither of them would want to put him or his new little family in danger.

What really worried him was that he had had no news from back home since they left. He was hoping that they'd give him some kind of update, but he wasn't sure if they had figured out that he was a part of the plan to get Rovena out of Albania, or if they just had no news to give.

He quickly got their bags into the SUV that Edon had waiting for them as Rovena watched him with her bags. "Are you worried that I'm going to forget your shoe bag?" he teased.

"Maybe," she said, "and, it's a boot bag."

"Right," he breathed, helping her into the passenger side of the car. "I'm sure that your high-heeled boots will come in handy out in the middle of nowhere, princess."

"Well, you won't be around to see how handy they come in while I'm in Colorado," she spat.

"Actually, I will be," he said. Rovena didn't know about the conversation that he had with Edon or the fact that the Tirana family had followed them to America. They had to make sure that they weren't being followed, which meant that they'd be taking a detour to Bekim's place, and he'd be with her the whole way.

"What do you mean by that?" she asked. "I thought you were supposed to deliver me to my brother's place and then, head back to Albania," she said, reciting the plan back to him.

"I know that was the plan, but it's been changed," he said. "Edon called while you were freshening up in the bathroom after we landed. He said that a Tirana jet took off just after we did, and he doesn't want us going straight to Bekim's house."

"Is he worried that we're being followed?" she asked.

"Yes, but you don't have to worry. I'll take care of you, Rovena," he promised.

She barked out her laugh and he tried to figure out what he had said that was funny. "I'm pretty sure that I've proven that I can take care of myself, Jak. I mean, you saw what I did to your cousin, right?" she asked.

"I did, and I understand that you can take care of yourself," he assured. "But you also can't go off and kill people here in America. You'll end up in prison and your brothers won't be able to ride into your rescue."

"I don't need them to rescue me either," she spat. He could tell that he wasn't getting anywhere with her, and Jak learned a long time ago that arguing with Rovena never ended well for him.

"Listen, if you don't like the new plan, you should call your brother and tell him. I'm just helping Edon out and doing as he ordered," Jak insisted.

"So, you're just following orders then?" she asked.

"Correct," he agreed. "And if you have an issue with it, call Edon and complain to him."

"Fine," she spat, pulling her cell phone from her purse. "I will." She had her brothers wrapped around her finger, but Jak was sure that they'd never do anything to put her in danger. Edon would set her straight and Jak was secretly going to enjoy watching that happen.

Edon answered immediately as if he was expecting his sister's call. Jak almost felt bad for the guy for the shit that Rovena was going to give him.

"Hello, Rovena," Edon answered. "I'm guessing that you don't care that it's the middle of the night over here, right?" he asked.

"Not at all," she said. "Why am I not going to see Bekim?" she asked.

"Because it's not safe. You've been followed and I've given Jak orders that he needs to lead whoever followed you to the States on a chase."

"So, I'm being used as bate to lead the Tirana's away from Bekim. Do I have that right?" she spat.

"Well, when you say it like that, little sister, you make it sound worse than it really is," Edon insisted. Jak sat back and watched the two Garo siblings go back and forth. He enjoyed watching the Garo brothers try to square off with their little sister since Rovena usually won every battle with her brothers.

"Don't call me that, and don't diminish what's happening here," she said. "I just want answers, Edon. Can you give me a straight answer?"

"I think I already have. You can't go to Bekim's place because it's not safe. Jak knows how to lose the tail on you guys, let him do that, and then, you can go visit our brother."

She sighed, "Fine," she spat. He knew that Bekim and his new family's safety would change her mind about heading to her brothers. She would want to keep them safe, even if it meant that she didn't get what she wanted.

"I promise that as soon as it's safe, I'll let you know," Edon assured.

"Thank you," she breathed.

"Tell Jak I'll be in touch," Edon said and ended the call.

"Here," she spat, holding his phone back at him. Jak took the phone from her, and she crossed her arms, and sat back in her seat.

"I'm sorry that he didn't tell you what you wanted to hear," Jak said. "But keeping your family safe is Edon's top priority."

"And you don't think that it's my top priority too?" she asked.

"That's not what I said," he insisted. Jak sighed and quickly looked Rovena over. She was always giving him a fight—even when they were kids. He wondered if she'd ever cut him a break. "Can we not fight about every little thing?" he breathed.

"I'm not fighting with you," she said.

"Everything becomes a fight with you, honey. Even when I agree with you, you find a way to turn it around and start a fight with me," he said. "Hell, this is the first honest conversation that we've had with each other in years and you're twisting my words all around. Can't we just try to get along?"

"No," she whispered.

"Why the hell not?" he shouted.

"Because if I agree to get along with you, that will mean that I have to let my guard down, and I can't do that around you," she said.

"I'd never do anything to hurt you, Rovena," he promised.

"You already have," she breathed, "you broke my heart, Jak."

"I didn't have any choice in how things ended with us, Rovena." She was just fourteen and he was sixteen when the war between their families broke out. He had been best friends with her brothers, especially Bekim. And even though he wasn't proud of his behavior, he followed Rovena around like a lovesick puppy until his father ordered him not to have any contact with the Garo family members anymore. Having to stay away from the Garos wasn't easy. Honestly, he broke his own heart not being able to hang around Rovena anymore. He had fallen in love with her and telling her that might have been purely selfish on his part, but he felt that not saying the words would be something that he regretted for the rest of his life.

"I hated the war between our family tearing us apart, but you and I didn't have any choice in the matter. It didn't change the way that I felt about you, Rovena." He was still in love with her, and Jak had a feeling that wasn't going to change any time soon. Especially now, when he was going to have to spend so much one on one time together.

"If I'm going to be forced to spend time with you, I don't want to talk about feelings and all of that crap, Jak," she spat. Rovena never liked to talk about feelings. When he told her that he was in love with her as a teen, she changed the subject and asked him if he'd drive her to the mall, since he had just gotten his license. He, of course, said that he would, but it still hurt to have her dismiss his sweeping declarations of love.

"Whatever you want, princess," he grumbled. He wanted to call her a chicken for pushing him off. He wanted to tell her to stop acting the coward and just accept the reality that they were meant to be together but pushing Rovena into anything never worked out for anyone doing the pushing. She usually pushed right back, and that would have made this road trip unbearable.

"Stop calling me that," she mumbled. Rovena looked out the passenger window, effectively ignoring him. Jak knew that she was done discussing feelings and anything else that he might come up with. Rovena was effectively shutting him out again, and that stung like a son of a bitch.

ROVENA

She wasn't sure where Jak was taking her or what they were going to do if the Tirana family caught up to them. Rovena could take care of herself, that much she was sure of, but Jak was going to have to deal with his own family members trying to kill not only her but him now too. As soon as he agreed to help her escape Albania and the Tirana family coming after her, he put a target on his own back. His family wouldn't care what his last name was—he was now public enemy number one.

Rovena hated that he was giving up his life for her. If she was being honest, she still felt the same way about him as she did when they were kids. She was only fourteen when she started to notice him, but she had no idea what to do about her feelings. With only her father and brothers to talk to, she couldn't ask them for their advice. If her father had any clue that she had a crush on Jak Tirana, he would have forbidden her from seeing him ever again.

She loved the way that Jak followed her around, even if she pretended not to notice him. Without her mother around to give her advice about boys, she had to take matters into her own hands. Rovena couldn't remember where she had read the article, but when she was about fifteen, she picked up a magazine that told her to ignore the boy she liked, to get his attention. Boy, did it work too. Jak seemed to follow her around even more when she started to ignore him. Gone were the days when she'd beg him to spend some time with her, even asking him to drive her to the mall. No, she followed the magazine article's advice to ignore the boy, and she never looked back. Not until it was too late.

Their families had gone to war when she was almost fifteen and Jak was lost to her. The boy who spent every spare minute at her family home, hanging out with her brothers, and trying to get her attention, was banished from her life. Her father had given the order that they were no longer allowed to spend time with Jak, and it felt as though she was losing a piece of herself. Her brothers seemed to move on without him in their lives, easily fulfilling their roles in the Garo family, but she couldn't do the same. He was gone and that broke her heart.

They drove the rest of the day in near silence, only stopping for food, gas, and bathroom breaks. By the time Jak decided to stop for the night, her whole body ached, and she wasn't even sure what state they were in. "Where are we?" she asked.

"Somewhere outside of Chicago," Jak said.

"I thought that Chicago was a big city. At least, that's how it looks in the movies. Where are all the big buildings?"

She looked around in the darkness and back at Jak. "I mean, there's a cow right over there," she said, pointing to the farm field that butted up to the hotel's parking lot.

"I said outside of Chicago. I believe that most of Illinois is rural," Jak said.

"Will we even get to see the city?" she asked.

He shrugged, "No idea," he admitted. "No, grab your suitcase with all of your ridiculous boots in it."

"They aren't ridiculous," she insisted. She was sick of him giving her shit about her boots. She only had a few minutes to pack and most of her belongings were strewn across her apartment. Packing anything was pure luck on her part.

"Whatever you say, honey. Just grab your bag and let's get out of the cold." She tugged her suitcase and bag from the trunk and followed him into the lobby. The hotel, if that's what the run-down place could be called, looked like it had seen better days. It looked more like a motel, and she wondered if she'd be able to have a decent hot shower in the place or a clean bed to sleep in.

Jak checked in using a fake name and accent that if Rovena was being honest, kind of turned her on. She wondered when he practiced his American accent and how he had gotten so good at it. Jak asked for one room, and she cleared her throat. "Um, two rooms please," she corrected. The poor guy behind the desk looked between the two of them as if trying to decide who to listen to.

"We only need one room," Jak insisted.

"I'm not sleeping in the same bed as you," she whispered.

"I don't give a fuck where you sleep," he said. He turned back to the guy behind the desk who was still staring them down. "Give us just a second," he said. Jak grabbed her arm and walked her across the lobby, and she huffed out her breath.

"You're blowing this for us. We need to get in and out of these places without notice if this is going to work. My cousins could be right on our asses and you're standing here arguing with me about whether we need one or two rooms. I can't keep you safe if you are in a separate room."

"Do I need to remind you again that I don't need you to keep me safe, Jak?" she spat.

"Not at all," he assured. "But I promised your brother that I'd keep an eye on you and I can't do that from another room. My x-ray vision isn't working," he joked.

"Fine, I'll stay in the same room with you, but you're sleeping on the floor," she insisted.

"That won't be necessary," he said. "I'll just get us two beds. No need for either of us to sleep on the floor, princess." God, he wasn't going to give up calling her that, and she was sure that Jak would do anything to piss her off.

"Fine," she spat. "Just get the room. I'm exhausted and want a shower."

"Of course, your royal highness," he teased. She rolled her eyes at him and followed Jak back over to the front desk. "We'll take one room," he repeated. The guy looked past Jak at her and Rovena nodded her agreement.

"Great," he said. "I have you in room twelve."

"It has two beds, right?" Rovena asked as he handed Jak the key to the room.

"Oh, sorry, but all our rooms are single bedrooms. All queens," the guy said. Shit, she was going to have to go full-on bitch and insist that Jak sleep on the floor after all, but there was no way that she'd sleep in the same bed with him.

"You can't be serious," she grumbled.

"You'll be fine, honey," Jak insisted. She didn't feel fine. Nothing about this felt fine. She had spent the past few years trying to avoid Jak and now, she was going to have to spend the night in the same room and possibly, the same bed as him.

She followed him back outside and around the corner to their room. "I've never stayed in a place like this," she admitted.

"I can't imagine that you have, princess," he said. "I mean, you're used to luxury and this place is run down." They walked to their room, and he helped her finish dragging her suitcase full of shoes up to the second floor to the room with the giant black "12" painted on the door. "This place doesn't even have an elevator," Jak grumbled.

"You could have chosen a nicer place," she breathed, lugging her bag up the stairs behind her.

"That's exactly where my family will be looking for us, princess. I'm betting that they'll check all the swanky places first," he said. He was right. The Tiranas would check all the nice places first before looking for her in a crappy place like this. It was actually a smart move, bringing her here.

He opened the door to the room and helped her in, shoving their bags in after her. Rovena quickly looked around after he flicked on the lights and honestly, it was worse than she had imagined. The place was a complete dump and the single queen size bed that sat in the middle of the room looked way too small for two grown people.

"I know that it looks bad, but it's only for one night," he

assured. "Then, we'll get back on the road. I just need a few hours of sleep. You can take the bed and I'll take the floor." She looked at the dingy carpet and back up at him.

"Tell me that you're up to date on your tetanus shots," she teased. "I wouldn't let my dog sleep on that floor."

"I've slept in worse places," he admitted. Rovena felt bad knowing that he was going to have a horrible night's sleep on the floor. If he was going to spend the next few days driving them around in circles to lose their tail, she wanted him fresh and ready to focus.

"You can take the bed," she insisted. "You need sleep more than I do. I'll sleep out in the car."

"Absolutely not," he shouted. "I won't be able to keep you safe if you're out in the car. That defeats the whole purpose of stopping for the night. If you sleep in the car, I sleep in the car."

"Well, that's just stupid," she shouted back. "You just said that you need a good night's sleep and I'm giving you the option for one."

"It's not an option," he insisted. "Listen, you take the bed. I'm fine with sleeping on the floor." She sighed, knowing that she wouldn't win this argument. There was only one way around both of their issues.

"We can both sleep on the bed," she said.

"You don't have to do that," he insisted.

"We're both adults, Jak. We can both get a good night's sleep in the same bed without it being awkward. We're just two old friends, sleeping side by side, trying to rest up for the long journey ahead."

"You've always been too dramatic, honey," he teased. Jak used to love to tell her that she missed her calling to be on stage because she loved to make everything more dramatic than it needed to be. Maybe it was the fact that she was the only girl in the family or that her brothers liked to encourage her, but she did love drama—just not when it involved the Tirana family coming after her.

JAK

Jak wasn't sure if agreeing to share a bed with Rovena was a dream come true or if it was going to be his worst nightmare. He had agreed that they could both be adults and that he could keep his hands to himself, but he just wasn't sure if that was true. The one thing that he was sure of was that he'd be taking many cold showers to keep his unruly cock under control.

Rovena came out of the bathroom, having showered, and slipped into a pair of shorts and a T-shirt that made him want to swallow his tongue. "Tell me that you brought warmer pajamas," he said.

She smiled and looked down at her skimpy pajamas. "You don't like my pajamas?" she asked. He more than liked her pajamas. He fucking loved them, but that wasn't the point. "It's cold in Colorado," he reminded.

"Well, I usually sleep naked, so this is a step up. I'm sure that I'll be fine, once we finally get to Colorado." Jak knew that she was angry with him for not taking her directly to her brother, but he had to admit, he was enjoying his one-on-one time with her—not that it would change anything between the two of them. Rovena had made it crystal clear that she wasn't interested in him.

"Don't pout, honey," he breathed. Jak picked up his clothes and toiletries and walked to the bathroom. "It doesn't suit you." He shut the bathroom door to her protesting that she wasn't pouting, and he almost wanted to laugh. She was the most stubborn woman he'd ever known, and it was probably the thing he loved most about her.

Jak took his time in the shower, getting himself off not once, but twice, before brushing his teeth and heading back out to find Rovena tucked into her side of the bed. She had rolled the blankets under her body, as if she was making herself into a burrito, and left him the spare blanket to cover up with. The best part of the whole scene was she was pretending to be asleep, and he couldn't help but laugh.

"Well, since you're already asleep, I'm sure you won't mind if I slip into bed naked then," he loudly whispered.

"I would very much mind," she said, not bothering to open her eyes.

"I knew that you weren't sleeping," he said.

Rovena peeped an eye open and sat up. "And I knew that you weren't naked." He was betting she had no idea that he was wearing a pair of gym shorts, but that was all he had on. She looked him over, from head to toe, and he had to admit, he liked it. This was the first time she had shown any interest in him in a damn long time.

"Where is your shirt?" she asked.

"I didn't have time to pack much before we left. You're

lucky that I'm wearing shorts right now. I don't have pajamas," he said.

"I see," she breathed, "we're going to have to do some shopping then to make sure that you don't freeze to death on our way to Colorado. I guess it's a good thing that you won't have to stick around once we get to my brothers."

"Why wouldn't I stick around?" he asked.

"You can't be serious," she said, rolling over to face him. "Once you deliver me to Bekim, you'll be free to go. I won't need a babysitter anymore." He hadn't really given that part of his plan much thought, but the idea of leaving Rovena alone in the states, even if she'd have her brother around, didn't sit well with him.

"I'm not here to babysit you, Rovena," he spat. "I'm here to keep you safe and even take care of you."

"And as we have already discussed, I don't need you to do either of those things for me," she insisted. God, she was so stubborn, it was infuriating.

"Fine, believe what you want, I just can't leave you," he said. "Besides, if I left you with Bekim, where would I go? I can't go home now. My family won't believe that I was acting against my will by helping you. I've already been marked a traitor and I can never go back to Albania." Neither of them could, but he wouldn't share that bit of information with her yet.

"I'm sure that you'll find someplace to settle down. Don't you want a wife and kids someday?" she asked. It was a loaded question for him because he did want those things. He just wanted them with Rovena.

He shrugged, "Can we talk about this in the morning?" he asked. "I'm suddenly feeling very tired." He slipped into bed next to her, tugging some of the covers away from her.

"So, that's how it's going to be?" she asked. "I ask you a simple question that you don't want to answer, and you're going to ignore me and go to sleep."

"Yes," he breathed, turning over to give her his back.

"I guess you just can't handle the tough stuff. I mean, I didn't have you pegged for a coward, Jak," she taunted. He knew that he was falling for her ploy to get him to talk, but he was. He turned over and stared her down.

"I'm not the coward, here, honey," Jak spat.

"And what does that mean?" Rovena asked, inching a little bit closer.

"It means that every time I bring up the fact that I have feelings for you, you run away or change the topic," he said. Jak was done playing the fool. He was going to lay everything out for her and let the chips fall where they may. It was now or never. "I love you," he breathed. She stood and shoved the covers off her body, crossing the hotel room to put some distance between the two of them. He could always tell if she was nervous about something, she usually wore a path in the floor pacing.

"Don't say that to me if you don't mean it, Jak," Rovena whispered. He meant every single word, but from the look on her face, she wouldn't believe him for a second.

"I can't make you believe me, Rovena," he admitted. "But I meant what I said."

"I know that you think that you love me, but you don't know me anymore, Jak. You used to know me, but then, you stopped coming around and now, you can't claim to love me."

"Sure I can, because I do. I love you, Rovena. And don't make it sound like I chose to walk away from you. I was ordered to. You know that I can't go up against my uncle." He never went up against his uncle because he knew his place. Since his parents were killed, his uncle had taken him in and given him everything he'd need to be able to keep going. He had a roof over his head and food in his belly, and he knew that if he stepped one foot out of bounds, he'd be on the street, or worse.

"We could have found a way to see each other, if you really wanted to see me, Jak."

"No, we couldn't have," he insisted. "My uncle would have found out about me sneaking around to see you and your brothers. I'd love to say that I had the nerve to go up against him, but I don't. If I would have tried to see you, it would have only gotten us both killed." He couldn't put her in danger and sneaking to see her and her brothers would have put them all in danger. His uncle was always watching and waiting for him to fuck up. He was harder on Jak than he was the rest of the guys and that had everything to do with the bad blood between his uncle and his parents. He often wondered if his uncle was somehow responsible for his parents' deaths.

"I can't go back now, Jak," she said. "Our last names haven't changed. We're still the same people we were, and our families are still at war." That all was true, but he had an ace up his sleeve.

"I agree, and that's why I've come up with a plan," he said. She stopped pacing long enough to look him over and he couldn't help his smile.

"You have a plan?" she asked.

"Yep, I have a plan," he proudly announced. "I think that we should change your name."

She shook her head at him. "That won't matter, Jak. I'm pretty sure that the Tirana family knows who I am by now. Changing my name won't help me to hide from them." Yeah, she wasn't getting it yet, but she would. He thought about how he wanted to do this, and knowing Rovena, she'd hate a grand sweeping romantic gesture, so he opted for short and simple.

"You should marry me and change your name to Tirana. They won't come after you if you're one of their own."

"Marry you?" she asked. "Jak, you can't be serious."

"Oh, I'm deadly serious. If we can convince my uncle that we ran away because we were in love, and wanted to get married, he might call off my cousins," Jak said.

"You're forgetting one very important part, Jak," she said. "I killed his oldest son. Your uncle will never let me go now." She was right, but his plan might be the only one to keep both of them alive.

"It's worth a try," Jak insisted. "Unless you have a better idea, I say we go with mine." His plan would finally give him everything that he ever wanted—namely, Rovena.

ROVENA

Hearing Jak say that he still loved her had her heart racing. She was sure that he had forgotten all about her once their families parted ways. To protect her heart, Rovena learned to pretend that she didn't care about him, but she still did. She had loved Jak since she was a kid, but she never imagined that he'd ask her to marry him.

Jak sat on the bed, staring her down as if expecting her to give him an answer. "I don't have a better idea," she admitted, "but, I also don't think that getting married is a good plan either." Jak looked just about as uncertain about the plan as she felt.

"If we get married, we'd have the protection of both of our families. The Tirana's might stop coming for you if you're one of them," he said.

"Might stop," she repeated his words. "It's not a guarantee, Jak. We could be getting married for nothing." Rovena noted the hurt in his eyes and hated that she made him feel that way again. That was all she seemed capable of doing to Jak—hurting him.

"It wouldn't be for nothing to me," he insisted. "I've already told you that I love you, Rovena. I'm not asking you to marry me solely to keep you safe. Tell me that you don't have feelings for me too," he said. She couldn't do that without lying to him. She still had feelings for him. She was still in love with him. The question was—should she tell him?

"I do have feelings for you, Jak," she whispered, sitting on the edge of the bed. He pulled her against his body, and God, it felt good to be held by him.

"Thank you for admitting that, honey," he said.

"It doesn't change anything," she said. "Our families are still at war, and we aren't allowed to be together."

"Yet, here we are," he breathed, "together." He was right and the tighter he held her, the more she wanted what he said to really be true.

"If I agree to marry you, Jak, we won't ever be able to go back home," she said. She knew that it would only serve to piss off both of their families once they all found out about the two of them getting married. Her brother wouldn't be happy about it either, but nothing she did ever seemed to please Edon.

"But we might be safe here," he said. "If we get married, I can convince my uncle to stop sending his guys after us. You'll have immunity and be under my protection."

"Even after I killed his son?" she asked.

"Yes," he promised, "my uncle lives by the old ways, and he'll honor our union."

"You make it sound so technical and easy," she grumbled.

"Because to our families, it will be that way. They don't need to know how we feel about each other, Rovena. To them, they'll believe that I married you to keep you safe and your brother will probably think the same, but I'm hoping that Edon comes around at some point." She hoped the same, but she wasn't so sure. Edon was the head of the Garo family and he'd have to follow the same rules that Jak's uncle did.

"So, what do we do now?" she asked.

"Well, tomorrow, we'll find a justice of the peace and get married. Then, I'll call to tell my uncle our good news," Jak said.

"What if our good news only makes him angry?" she asked.

"Then, we'll handle it together. We're a team now. But I don't think that will be the case," he promised. "Do you trust me?" he asked. She did, with her life, but admitting that was easier said than done.

"We're doing this then?" she asked. "We're going to pretend to be in love and get married just to keep your uncle off our backs?" she asked. She was pushing him for more. Hell, she was practically begging him for it, but she was too much of a chicken to come right out and ask him for more.

"We're not pretending to be in love," he insisted. "I've already admitted that I'm in love with you. I have been my whole life. And I know that you're in love with me too, you just don't want to admit it."

"How do you know that I'm in love with you?" she

asked. She wanted to challenge him; to tell him that he was wrong, but she couldn't. She was in love with him, whether she said those words out loud or not.

"I see it in your beautiful, brown eyes," he whispered, pulling her into his body. Rovena couldn't help herself; she wrapped her arms around his neck and let Jak hold her. It felt right to be in his arms—like being home after a very long trip.

"You do?" she asked.

"I do," he whispered. "Say that you'll marry me, but not because you want me to keep you safe. Tell me that you love me, Rovena." He was asking her for more than just her words. He was asking her for her heart and for some crazy reason, Rovena was all too willing to give it to him.

"I want to marry you because I love you, Jak," she breathed. He tugged her up his body and crushed his lips over hers. "What was that?" She panted when he broke the kiss.

"That was me showing you how much I love you, honey," Jak said.

"I can think of a few more ways for you to show me how much you love me, Jak," she whimpered. Rovena was all but begging the man for sex, but she didn't care. It had been so long since she had a man kiss her the way that Jak just had.

"I can too," he growled, lifting her into his arms to cross the room and toss her onto the bed. He was rough and she loved that about him. Jak never treated her like a princess even though he liked to tease her and call her one. He never acted as if her worth was wrapped up in shopping and frivolous events. He saw her and right now, that meant everything to her.

"Tell me now if you want me to stop, honey," he demanded.

"I don't want you to stop, Jak. I want this—I want you." It was the most honest thing she had ever said to anyone. She did want him with every fiber of her being and letting him go now wasn't an option. She wanted to be his in every way possible.

Jak kissed his way down her body, removing her clothes as he went. By the time he was finished with her, she was naked and panting for air. Rovena felt needy, wet, and ready for whatever he wanted from her next.

"I need to taste you," he whispered against her tummy. Rovena couldn't do anything but moan her approval. The thought of him putting his mouth on her girl parts did wicked things to her and being able to speak wasn't one of them.

Jak chuckled and slid down her body, settling between her legs. Rovena closed her eyes tight as if preparing herself for the onslaught of pleasure that Jak was sure to give her.

"Watch me, honey," he ordered. She peeped an eye open to look down her body. Jak was looking back up at her; the desire in his dark eyes was enough to make her self-combust. "Good girl," he praised before dipping his head into her girl parts to lick through her slick folds. Dear God—the man had a skilled tongue that had her singing out his name and begging him not to stop in seconds flat. By the time he finally finished with her, she felt like a wrung-out wash rag.

But Jak wasn't done with her. He tugged her limp body to the edge of the bed, quickly stripped, and slid into her without any warning. He took what he wanted from her, and it was perfect since she was willing to give him everything.

"You are so fucking beautiful, Rovena," Jak growled. He pumped in and out of her body, setting a punishing pace until she was shouting out his name again. Jak cried out to her and collapsed on top of her after spilling his seed deep inside her body.

She was his now—his and no one else's, and that worked for Rovena since a part of her had been his her entire life.

Rovena was getting sick of spending nights in shitty motels and running from the men who were supposedly following them. What if no one was after them and they were living this hell for no reason? All she wanted to do was get to Bekim's place and settle in before winter was upon them. Her brother liked to tell her how brutal winters were in Colorado, and honestly, she couldn't wait to be snowed into a little cabin with Jak.

He stayed true to his word and found a justice of the peace the day after he came up with the plan for the two of them to be married. It wasn't supposed to be romantic, but to Rovena, it was. She was marrying the man she had always dreamed of spending her life with since she was just a girl. Jak had even picked up wedding bands for the two of them at a little secondhand shop and when he slipped hers onto her finger, she felt as though she finally found her place in life. She was his wife, even if it was just a ploy to keep them both safe from his uncle. Rovena felt like she belonged to Jak and that made the day even more special.

Each night, Jak would hold her after they made love, in the crappy little motel room and promise her that everything was going to be okay. He said that he'd take care of her and for the first time in her adult life, Rovena wanted to let someone keep that promise to her. Sure, she had given up the high life in Albania where every night was a party and every good-looking man in the club would make her pretty promises—but she knew Jak would keep them.

Her favorite was the one where he promised her that they could settle down in a little cabin near her brother and sister-in-law. He said that he'd buy her a cabin and she could make it into their home, and the dream of that happening was what kept her going. Rovena imagined them growing old together in that cabin—maybe even raising a family, but she was getting ahead of herself.

Jak, of course, made good on that promise, buying her a cabin just down the road from her brother's place. She loved it and wanted to make it a home for them both. It was nice being close to family again and Jak had kept every promise that he had made to her along the way. She was no longer holding her breath, waiting for his uncle's men to catch up with them. Sure, they would always be a threat, but Rovena was learning to live each day happy to be with her new husband in Colorado.

She looked down from the ladder where she was hanging curtains as Jak walked into the room holding his cell phone. Rovena didn't like the look on his face. It was the same one he got every time there was trouble. "What's wrong?" she asked.

"Nothing," he lied, "need some help with those?" he asked, nodding to the curtains that were half hung.

"No," she breathed, stepping down from the ladder. "What I need is for you to be honest with me and tell me what's going on. We're a team, remember?" It was what he had promised her the first night that they were together.

"I remember," he said, "but I hate to worry you. You've seemed so happy these past few months."

"Well," she said, crossing the room to wrap her arms around his neck. "That's because I am happy. You've made me happy, Jak."

"I like hearing that," he whispered, dipping his head to gently kiss her lips. "I'd like to try to make you even happier if you'll let me." He bobbed his eyebrows at her, making her laugh.

"Jak," she breathed, "you are trying to distract me from our original conversation. What is going on?"

He sighed and reached into his pocket, pulling out his cell phone to hand to her. "Your brother, Edon texted," he said. "Apparently, my uncle has put a price on my head now as well as yours."

"I'm sorry that happened, but we both knew that it would only be a matter of time before he'd figure out that you weren't on his side of things, right?" Rovena asked.

"Yes, but I was hoping for some more time. This just means that we'll have to be extra careful. I don't want you going into town without me, got it?" he asked.

Rovena nodded, "Got it."

"I'm going to install extra security measures," he insisted.

"But this place is already more secure than a bank," Rovena teased. "What else can you do?"

"I can add more sensors and cameras," he said. "It's a good idea to keep us safe."

"I agree, but I think you have things pretty secure around here, Jak," she said. "Did Edon say that your uncle has sent any more men after us?" she asked.

"No," Jak breathed, "but, he will. It's only a matter of time before he does." She knew that was true. The Tiranas would stop at nothing to find Rovena. She had killed the heir to the throne and in doing so, she put a black mark on her back for the rest of her life. There was no way that she'd ever be able to go back to Albania. Even in America, she'd have to constantly look over her shoulder to make sure that no one was coming for her. Now, Jak would face the same fate, because of her, and that made her sad for them both.

JAK

Jak woke to a message on his cell phone from his cousin, Teodor. He wanted to meet to discuss the murder of his brother, Ari. He gave a local address and Jak knew that their time was up. His uncle had found them and sent his son to collect him and kill Rovena. He couldn't allow that, so he made up some bullshit story to tell Rovena about having to run into town. He'd find out what his cousin wanted, even though he had a pretty good idea already, and then, he'd find a way to keep Rovena safe from his family. He had made her that promise, and Jak planned on keeping it.

He quickly dressed and drove into town to the address that Teodor had given him in the long text message that he had left on his phone. It was an abandoned strip mall and just looking at the old place, covered in snow, gave Jak the creeps. He parked around back and walked into the last building on the left, as was instructed, to find his cousin standing in the back of the long, dark room.

"I'd say that it's good to see you, cousin, but it would be a lie since finding out that you married the bitch who killed my brother. Do you have any idea what your betrayal has done to our family?" Teodor asked. He had a pretty good idea what his walking away did to the Tirana Syndicate. It probably had a couple of their guys thinking about doing the same and his uncle would be left to worry about who was loyal, and who was a traitor.

When the Garo and Tirana families started this war, they both knew that there was no end in sight. But a few of the guys had loved ones on both sides, much like Jak did. He loved the Tirana family as though they were his own, and now, he was legally a part of them. If some of his uncle's guys decided to choose family and friends over loyalty to the family, that would cause some major problems in the syndicate.

"I didn't mean to cause the family or my uncle any problems. I just couldn't let him murder the woman that I love," Jak said. He was being truthful about that. He loved Rovena and keeping her safe was his top priority.

"She's the enemy. You knew that but you still fell in love with her?" his cousin asked.

"Rovena wasn't the enemy when I fell in love with her," he admitted. "That happened when we were just kids before the war between our families broke out. I stayed away from her all these years, but my feelings for her didn't change. I couldn't let your father hurt her. This vendetta needs to end, Teodor. She's my wife now." He hoped to play to his cousin's emotions and hope like hell that it worked, but from the look on Teo's face, his speech had proven ineffective.

"You really are a moron," his cousin accused, "you've given up everything for a Tirana, and now, you'll end up paying the ultimate price. My father wants you both back in Albania. I'm bringing you in, Jak." There was no way in hell that he'd allow that to happen. He just needed to come up with a damn good plan and fast.

"What about a deal?" Jak asked.

"What about a deal?" his cousin asked. "It's a bit too late to make a deal with the family, Jak. You had your chance to make the right decision and when you chose that bitch over the family, you lost." He didn't feel as though he had lost anything. Rovena was the best prize he'd ever won in his life. Jak knew that he was down to his last shot at getting both Rovena and him out of town alive. His cousin wasn't going to let either of them live—not after what Rovena had done to his brother.

"I know that you're mourning Ari," Jak said. "But bringing me and Rovena home to die won't bring him back."

"That bitch murdered him in cold blood," Teodor shouted.

"Because that's what Ari had planned for her. Rovena was acting in self-defense, and you know it." He could tell by the look on his cousin's face that he knew the truth. Ari was a wildcard, and he didn't always follow directions. He was supposed to bring Rowena into the Tirana headquarters. Instead, he chased her into an abandoned warehouse and threatened to kill her. What choice did she have but to shoot the guy—twice?

"Don't get in the middle of this, Jak. You're already in enough hot water. Hand her over and maybe, my father will look past your disloyalty, and you'll be able to come home." Jak knew for certain that his cousin was lying through his teeth. He would never be welcome back home, not that he'd want to go back. His place was with Rovena and if she wanted to stay in Colorado, to be closer to her brother, Bekim, then that's where he'd stay. Teo was just trying to get Jak to give up Rovena's location, and he wouldn't do that—ever.

"Okay, how about a trade then?" he offered. He knew how valuable he still was to his uncle. When Jak's parents died, they left him very well off, and along with the money, he also had a number of the Tirana family members who would stand by him in a pinch. They'd even go against his uncle to do so, at least that was what he was counting on.

"What kind of trade?" Teo asked.

"My life and everything that I bring to the Tirana family, for Rovena's. I want my uncle's personal guarantee that he won't go after her once I'm back in Albania, and in return, I'll give him my full backing."

"And why would he need you to back him?" Teo asked. "My father is the head of the Tirana Syndicate."

"As my father was before him," Jak reminded. He had grown up believing that he'd be the head of the Tirana family once his father stepped down, but his death left many uncertainties, including who would step up in his place. Jak was just a kid when his parents passed away, and his uncle used that fact to his advantage. He took the family from Jak, and honestly, he was fine with that. He never wanted to be the head of the Tirana Syndicate. He was just fine with living in the shadows—until now.

"Are you challenging my father?" Teo spat, taking a few menacing steps toward Jak.

"Not at all," Jak assured. "I'm just saying that I was in line for your father's seat on the throne. I no longer want it, but I still have a number of loyal backers in the family who would love to see me in a place of power. I can persuade them to step aside and give your father their full backing in return, all I ask is for Rovena's safety to be guaranteed."

Teo looked about ready to combust, he was so mad. "I'll have to make a phone call," he growled.

"I'm not going anywhere, cousin. I'm betting you have a few of the guys surrounding the building by now and if I even try to leave, I'm a dead man." From the smirk on Teo's face, he knew that he had guessed correctly. "I'll wait right here while you make your call." He pretended that he wasn't scared out of his mind with worry that his uncle would decline his offer and keep coming for Rovena. Jak might not have found a way out for them both, but at least, this way would give his wife a fighting chance.

The phone call between Teo and his father felt as though it took forever and when he finally ended the call and walked back into the room from the back alley, Jak felt like he was holding his breath waiting for the news. "Well?" he asked.

"You have a deal. You need to tell your new bride that you'll be leaving and will go back to Albania with me," he said. "My father has agreed to stop pursuing Rovena as long as she stays here, in America. If she comes home, all bets are off." He knew that never going home again would hurt

Rovena, but he was also sure that her brothers would sit on her if she tried to go back to Albania.

"How do I know that your father won't go back on his word once you get me home? How do I know that he just won't kill me and go after my wife again?" Jak asked.

"You don't know that for sure," Teo admitted. "But I'm a man of my word and I promise to have your back if things go south. You come home and work for the family—stay true to the Tirana Syndicate, and you won't have anything to worry about. You know me, cousin, and you know that my word is my bond." Jak did know that out of all his cousins, Teodor was the most upstanding one in the bunch. If he could trust any of them, it would be Teo.

"Fine," Jak said, "you have a deal." They shook hands and Jak felt as though he had just made a deal with the devil himself. Now, all he had to do was go back to his cabin, pack his shit, and tell his wife goodbye forever. He hated every part of this fucked up deal, but it was the only one he could make that would keep Rovena safe.

"I'll meet you at the local airport in one hour. Don't be late, or the deal is off. Don't make me come to find you and your pretty wife, cousin," Teo said. There was no way that he'd let that happen. Jak planned on being on that plane in one hour—it was the only way to keep the woman he loved safe.

Jak knew that if he didn't walk away from Rovena now, he never would. He needed to make a clean break and then, he'd find his way back to Albania where his uncle was waiting for him. It was part of the deal he had made with his family. He'd return home to serve the Tirana family again and Rovena would be safe. They promised to leave her alone. He was basically trading his life for hers, and he was fine with that as long as Rovena would have a life.

Jak pulled up to the cabin, which he now thought of as home, and cut the engine. He just sat there in his SUV and stared into the front windows, trying to come up with the words that he needed to tell the woman he loved that he was leaving her. There were no correct words to say and no good way to do any of this. He was just going to have to go into their cabin and break both of their hearts. It was the only way.

Jak walked into the cabin, knowing that this might be the last time he'd ever do that simple feat. He found the place empty, guessed that Rovena was at her brother's house, and decided to use the few minutes he had to pack some of his things. He walked up to their bedroom and found his suitcase and bag in the back of the closet, quickly filling it with as many of his clothes as he could fit. By the time Jak got back downstairs, bags in hand, he found Rovena standing in the kitchen.

"Hey," she shouted to him. "What would you like for dinner tonight? I know that you like to tease me for my lack of culinary skills, but I've been getting some tips from my sister-in-law, and she says that I've become quite the cook. Want to give my latest dish a try?" she asked, holding up a wooden spoon.

"Um, I won't be here for dinner tonight," he admitted. "I have to leave, Rovena."

She put the spoon down and turned off the stove.

"Leave?" she questioned, walking down the hallway to meet him at the front door. "Where are you going?"

"I have to go home, Rovena," he said. "I'm going back to Albania. My cousin, Teodor found me today and he has no idea that you're here. I agreed to go back home to deal with my uncle."

"You can't do that," she insisted.

"I'm leaving you," he shouted, causing her to jump. He hated doing that to Rovena. She was usually so in control and confident—not the crying, shaking woman who stood before him. "We're over."

"What do you mean? You're leaving me?" Rovena asked. The break in her voice was nearly his undoing. "How can you stand there and tell me that we're over?" she asked. This was harder than he had imagined it would be. He didn't want to leave her, but if he didn't meet his cousin in the next hour, to head back to Albania to face his uncle, they'd both be as good as dead. He made a promise to Rovena and her brothers that he'd keep her alive and Jak planned on keeping that oath to them all. Turning himself over to his uncle was the only way to keep the woman he loved alive. That was what he needed to focus on now—keeping Rovena alive.

"I have to go back to Albania," he almost whispered again. "I've made a deal with my cousin, Teodor, and he's agreed to help me with my uncle. It's the only way, Rovena," he said, leaving out the part about it being the only way to keep her safe and alive.

"You made a deal with your cousin?" she shouted. "You're going to go back home and get yourself killed." She was probably right but admitting that now would only end up with her tagging along on his trip back home. He couldn't allow that. He needed her to be free and clear of all this mess.

"I made a mistake, Rovena," he said. "I should have never married you. I thought that if I had you, no one would be able to get to you, but I was wrong."

She swiped at the tears that spilled down her face. "You said that you loved me and that's why you wanted to marry me, Jak," she reminded.

"I know, but I only said what I needed to get you to marry me," he lied. God, seeing the hurt in her eyes nearly did him in. He wasn't going to be able to stand there for much longer and lie to her face. Sooner or later, he'd cave and tell her the truth, and that was something that he didn't have time for.

"You lied to me?" she shouted.

He nodded, "I did," he breathed. "I only got you to marry me to keep you safe and fulfill my promise to Edon. But everything has backfired, and I need to go back home now. If you stay here, close to Bekim, I think that you'll be out of my uncle's line of fire." Honestly, that was the only truth he had told her today. The deal with his uncle was he'd go home and face whatever punishment his uncle had planned for him and in return, the Tirana family would leave Rovena alone. All she had to do was stay in America, and she'd live a long life—one that he'd miss every second of because he was an idiot.

"I don't believe you, Jak," she insisted. She reached for him, and he quickly pulled away. If he allowed Rovena to touch him, he'd give into what he wanted and stay with her. Leaving her and lying to her was the only way.

"Honestly, I don't have time for this. My plane is leaving in less than an hour now. I'm sorry that this whole thing hurt you, Rovena. I didn't mean to do that. You should be glad to be rid of me," he insisted.

"I should be, shouldn't I?" she asked. Rovena crossed her arms over her chest and nodded. She was shutting down emotionally in front of his eyes and he was pretty sure that she was going to let him just walk out of her life. Why did getting what he wanted from her have to hurt so damn much?

Jak wasn't sure what the protocol was for leaving his wife. Rovena was the first woman he'd ever loved and walked away from. "I'll send papers for a divorce once I get settled in Albania," he offered. She nodded and stood silently in front of him. Jak knew that she wasn't going to give him much more than that. "I hope that you can find the happiness that you deserve, Rovena. I'm sorry that I couldn't give that to you."

"Couldn't or won't?" she asked. He wasn't going to respond to that because she wouldn't like his answer.

"Have a good life, Rovena," he whispered, leaning in to gently kiss her cheek. She didn't respond to his words or his kiss and when he picked up his bags to leave the cabin, he almost wanted her to stop him—but what good would that serve? They'd have to repeat this whole song and dance all over again because the bottom line was, Jak was doing this to keep Rovena safe and give her a future. He'd go home to his uncle and face whatever he had planned for him—whether it be working for the family or worse. Honestly, he wasn't sure that death was worse than working for the Gary Syndicate again, but he knew it would rate pretty high up there.

He stepped out into the snow and loaded his bags into the trunk of his waiting SUV. Jak didn't bother to look back to see if Rovena was watching him. He didn't want to know. It was taking all his strength to leave her and if he found her watching him, he'd break down and give up the fight. He was walking away from the only woman he'd ever loved and that just plain sucked.

ROVENA

Rovena lifted her head from the toilet seat and moaned. This was the fourth morning that she had run from the bed to the bathroom to be sick. Whatever stomach bug she had been cursed with was really kicking her ass.

When she finally felt well enough to get up from the bathroom floor, she made her way to the kitchen of her little cabin, bypassing the coffee machine, and going straight for the crackers. Maybe she just needed something in her stomach, and she'd feel better as she had the past few days. As soon as lunch time hit, she was hungry again and that gave her hope that she wouldn't wake up the next day and puke her guts into the toilet—but she was wrong.

Rovena texted her sister-in-law, Amra, and asked her if there was a doctor she'd recommend in town. She was going to have to try to get something to take away this nausea. Amra texted back right away with the name of her doctor and asked if she wanted her to run over some crackers and ginger ale. Rovena loved that her sister-in-law wanted to help, but the last thing she wanted to do was get her brother's family sick—especially with a newborn in the picture now. She texted back that she was well stocked and thanked Amra for the recommendation and offer to help. After Rovena made her doctor's appointment, she quickly showered and dressed, wanting to get to town to pick up a few things at the store before meeting her new doctor.

There was something about going to town that made her feel sad. Maybe it was because she and Jak had spent so much time in town together or maybe it was because she was hoping to run into him there. She wasn't even sure if Jak was still in town or if he had gone back to Albania. When he told her that it was over between the two of them, she was in shock and didn't ask questions. Instead, she stood there like a fool and just nodded her head. It was all she seemed capable of doing. Speaking would have led to crying and she didn't want to do that in front of him. No, she saved that for when she got back to their cabin.

Rovena planned on staying at their cabin until she could figure out her next move. Jak bought the place for her as a wedding gift and she hoped that he'd remember that and come back home to her, but she had a feeling that he wasn't planning on moving back to the cabin. He made it very clear that he didn't want her anymore. He told her that he only married her to keep her safe, and that felt like a knife to her gut. Everything that happened between the two of them couldn't have been fake. He wasn't pretending with her; she knew that for sure. Rovena could see it in his dark eyes, every time he looked at her—Jak loved her and there was a reason why he was giving her up now. She was sure that it had to do with his family, but she couldn't be certain. One thing she was sure of was that she wanted Jak back and she'd do just about anything to make that happen.

She parked in the back of the lot, hoping to avoid any unwanted attention, and hurried into the back door of the clinic. She told the receptionist her name and was told to fill out a bunch of forms. A nurse came out to collect her before she was even finished with the form and told her not to worry about the last page. She wanted to ask why she was even given the last page if she didn't have to fill it out but decided against sounding too snarky before her appointment. Rovena chalked up her current mood to being grumpy and still not feeling one hundred percent.

The nurse took her vitals and got her weight, telling her to have a seat on the very uncomfortable patient's bed that sat in the corner of the room. Rovena thanked her and tried to make herself comfortable, though she felt anything but. The doctor came in quickly and she was impressed by how efficient they were. Amra had warned her that they could get busy, and she might have to wait sometime before seeing the doctor.

The woman doctor asked her what felt like a thousand questions and when she got to the one about when her last period was, Rovena stared at her like a deer caught in the headlights. Shit—had she really missed her last period and didn't realize it? She quickly counted backward in her head and realized that she had missed her last period.

"I'm late," Rovena whispered.

"Okay, well, let's rule out pregnancy before we jump

Rovena

into a full panel of tests. Can you give us a urine sample?" the doctor asked.

"I believe that I can," Rovena agreed.

"Wait here and I'll get the nurse to bring you a sample cup. After your test results are ready, I'll come back in and give you them," the doctor said.

"I appreciate that," Rovena said, trying to act calm and feeling anything but. She watched as the doctor walked out of the room and heard her talking in muffled tones to whom Rovena assumed to be the nurse. Minutes later, the nurse came back into the examination room, smiling and holding up the tiniest cup Rovena had ever seen.

"I have to pee in that?" she asked.

"Yeah, it's not as hard as it looks," the nurse assured. She gave her quick instructions and told her to leave the half-full cup on the sink in the bathroom. She took the cup from the nurse, mumbling something about the cup being too small and the nurse giggled. Rovena found none of this funny—especially the fact that she might be pregnant with Jak's baby. How was she going to deal with everything if Jak still refused to talk to her?

"Don't be positive," she whispered to the cup full of pee as she sat it on the sink and washed her hands. She checked her reflection, noting that she looked about ready to break down in tears, and shook her head at herself. The last thing she wanted to do was break down in front of a bunch of strangers. She'd save that for when she got back to her cabin and had to decide what to do next.

She didn't have to wait long for the doctor to walk back into the tiny room and announce that she was pregnant. Rovena wanted to say that she was shocked, but once she realized that she had missed a period, she knew the truth. The morning sickness should have been her first clue, but she needed to make a trip to town to figure it all out. She was going to be a mother and Jak, a father. She just needed to find him to tell him and that was going to prove tricky.

As soon as she paid her bill and promised to make a follow-up visit with an OBGYN in town, she was on her way back to her cabin. There was no way that she'd be able to find Jak on her own, but she knew the man who'd be able to help her. Rovena just had to figure out how to not tell Edon that she was pregnant because the first person she wanted to tell was Jak. It was only right.

She dialed her brother's number and from his groggy voice answering on the other end, she knew that she had woken him up, and that made her feel like crap. "Sorry, did I wake you?" she asked, already knowing the answer.

"You did," he grumbled. "Do you have any idea what time it is here?"

"I do, and I said that I'm sorry, but I need your help. I have no one else to turn to."

"Does this have anything to do with Jak disappearing on you?" Edon asked.

"Who told you that Jak left me?" she asked.

"It doesn't matter. I'm sorry that you had to go through all of that. If it helps, I truly believe that he loved you, Rovena." She wanted to tell her brother that hearing him say that didn't help her, but she needed to play nice.

"He still does love me, Edon," she said. "He just needs a reminder. I need to find him. Can you help me do that?" she asked.

"As long as he wants to be found. If he's gone off-grid, I

might not have much luck. Give me a couple of days to try to track him down," Edon said.

"Thank you," she breathed. It was the first glimmer of hope that Rovena had felt in the few days since Jak had left her.

"I'll be in touch, sis," Edon promised, ending the call before she could thank him again. He didn't ask her why she needed to find him, and honestly, that was a relief. She had to figure out what she was going to do once she found Jak because right now, she had no idea.

She got home and took a hot shower, trying to calm her frazzled nerves. Rovena was going to have to call Bekim and tell him that she had gotten herself pregnant since she'd need his help to find Jak. She knew that he still had contacts in the Tirana family since marrying one of their own. Then, she was going to have to swear him to secrecy because there was no way that she'd want Edon to find out about the baby yet. Her older brother would try to control every aspect of her, and her baby's lives, and she couldn't allow that.

Rovena crawled into bed and pulled her blankets up over her body, finding her cell phone on the nightstand. She dialed her brother's number and he answered immediately. "I've heard about Jak," he said. "I'm going to kill that fucker."

"You are not," she insisted. "But that's not why I'm calling," she said. She knew that sooner or later, word would get back to both Edon and Bek that Jak had left her, but she just never imagined that it would be so quickly.

"Why are you calling then?" he asked.

"I need to tell you something, and I need you to promise that you won't tell Edon. Can you do that?" she asked. Rovena knew that Bek could keep secrets from his older brother. He had kept quite a number of them when he met his wife, who was also a Tirana.

"I don't like this, but I can keep a secret. As long as your life isn't in danger or any shit like that," Bekim said.

"It's not," she said, "but, it's about to change a whole lot in the next year. I just found out that I'm pregnant." She waited for the string of curses to stop on the other end of the call before continuing. "I need to find Jak to tell him, but I'm worried that it's not safe for me to go digging around. I won't put my baby in danger. I have more than myself to think about now."

"I'll find him and when I do, I'm dragging his ass home so we can both kill him," Bekim insisted.

"I don't want to kill him, Bek, I want to tell him that he's going to be a father." She left out the part where she also hoped that telling him the news would end with him wanting to come home. Jak was going to have to choose between his family and her. Rovena just hoped like hell that he'd chose her and the baby because if he didn't, she'd have to figure out how to raise a human being on her own.

"Are you okay?" Bekim calmed down enough to ask.

"I will be. This morning sickness is no joke," she breathed.

"How about you move in here with us for a few months?" Bek asked. "You can hang out here and we can help you get over the first trimester." She heard everything he wasn't saying out loud. If the Tirana Syndicate found out that she was pregnant with Jak's baby, they'd come for her. Tirana blood meant everything to them.

"Do you really think that they'll still come after me?" she asked. Jak had prided himself on putting in the best security system that he could find. She'd be safe, right?

"I have no idea what's going on here, sis. To be safe, I think that we should move you in here with me until I can hunt down Jak." Bekim seemed sure that he'd be able to find Jak, but Rovena wasn't as positive about the whole situation.

"He's in Albania," she almost whispered. "He told me that he was going home to work for his uncle."

"I hate to be the one to tell you this, but Jak never got on the plane to go back to Albania, Rovena. Edon heard about it from one of our guys on the inside of the Tirana Syndicate that the jet returned home without Jak on it. There was a problem with his cousin and I'm not really sure what happened from there, but Jak didn't go home to work for his uncle. In fact, his uncle has upped the price on Jak's head. He's not safe and I'm worried that you aren't either." This was the last thing she needed after the day she had already had. Finding out that she was pregnant with Jak's baby was stressful enough without adding to it that no one seemed to know where her long-lost husband was. One thing was perfectly clear to her—she'd have to move in with her brother if she wanted to keep herself and her unborn child safe. That was her top priority now.

"I appreciate you giving me the update, Bek. I will move in with you guys. I appreciate the offer, but I need you to make me a promise," she insisted.

"If I can, you know I will, sis," Bekim said.

"Just find Jak and bring him back to me," she whispered.

Two Weeks Later

"Do you think he's coming back?" she asked her brother Bekim. He held his son and she suddenly longed for something that she might never have. The thought of watching Jak hold their baby was becoming more of a dream and less of a reality.

"He's your husband," her brother reminded.

"Right, and he's been missing for two weeks now," she spat. It wasn't that he was really missing. Bekim had found him a few days ago and reported back to her. Jak was living one town over in a shady motel that reminded her of the one that they had stayed in together, on their first night in America. It was the night that he told her that he loved her and made her believe that his crazy plan of the two of them getting married could work. It was also the night that Rovena finally let her guard down and told Jak that she loved him too. Marrying him was the easy part. Telling their families turned out to be a nightmare. His family didn't seem to care what her last name was now, the Tirana's just wanted her head on a platter.

Bekim's wife, Amra, walked into the den and handed her an envelope. "This was just delivered for you," she said. Rovena pulled the envelope open and recognized Jak's handwriting right away.

"It's from Jak," she breathed.

"What does it say?" Bekim asked, handing his son over to Amra. "Is he okay?" Sometimes, she forgot that her brothers were friends with Jak. They had all lost Jak when the war broke out between their families, and they couldn't lose him again.

"He wants me to meet him at the gas station about two miles from our cabin," she said. She had moved out of their cabin as soon as she found out that she was pregnant. If the Tirana family came looking for her there, out in the middle of nowhere, she might not be able to protect herself and her unborn child. That wasn't acceptable to Rovena, so she moved in with Bekim, still keeping her secret to herself. It felt wrong to tell her brother about the baby before she told Jak but now was her chance. She'd meet with him and convince him to come home with her. If she had to use her baby as a way to persuade him, she would. Rovena would do anything to get her husband home with her—where he belonged.

"You can't go alone," Bekim insisted.

"He's my husband, as you have already pointed out, and I'm sure that I'll be safe," Rovena assured.

"At least let Bekim ride along with you and stay in the car, Rovena," Amra insisted. "Don't forget that I'm a Tirana too. If Jak is really working for them, they'll be very persuasive in getting him to have you meet with him. He might not be himself."

"Who else would Jak be then?" Rovena asked. "If he's in some kind of trouble, I owe it to him to help him out of it. I'm going to meet with my husband." She looked at her brother, worry etched on Bekim's face because of her. Rovena hated that she was putting her family through all this mess. "Fine, you can come with," she said, "but, you're staying in the car. You can be my lookout."

"Thanks, sis," Bekim said. "I knew that somewhere deep down, you could be reasonable."

"Oh, shut up," Rovena sassed. "Be ready to go in five minutes. We have twenty minutes until we need to meet Jak and I want to get there early to scope out the place. I don't want any surprises." She had already had enough of them. Her tummy roiled and she worried that she was going to be sick again, but there was no time for that. She was just going to have to have a talk with her tiny passenger and tell him or her that Mommy had to go rescue Daddy. Then, she'd find a way to tell Jak about the baby. It might be the only way to get him to come to his senses.

Bekim was waiting for her in the car by the time she grabbed her purse and coat. "You're late," he chided as she slipped into the passenger seat.

"I am not," she spat. "Here's the address," she said, handing him the note from Jak, telling her where to meet him.

"I know where the place is," Bekim said. "I don't like this Rovena. I have a bad feeling that we're walking into a trap. Who's to say that note is even from Jak?" he asked.

"I say it's from him. This looks like his handwriting," she said, nodding to the paper.

"What if he was forced to write that to you? What if he's in on whatever the Tirana's have planned for you?" She couldn't answer any of those questions for him. She had no idea what she'd do if any of that was true.

"I just need to see Jak," she breathed. "I have to talk to him and try to convince him to come home."

"Are you all right, sis?" Bekim asked. "You seem a bit out

of sorts." If her brother considered her being pregnant "Out of sorts" then she was definitely not all right.

"I just have a lot on my mind is all," she said. That wasn't a lie. She had the weight of the world on her shoulders right now and seeing Jak might fix everything for her. "I just need to see Jak," she whispered more to herself than to Bekim.

"I get that, but you have to be ready for the fact that he might not want to see you, sis. He might be meeting with you for closure. Are you going to be able to accept that and walk away from him, if that's what Jak asks you to do?" She'd never be able to accept that Jak didn't want her anymore. Was she so easy to dispose of for him? If he wanted closure, she'd give him one hell of a fight.

"No," she said. "I won't accept the fact that he could walk away from me so easily. He didn't marry me to keep me safe, Bek, he married me because he loves me."

"I know," Bekim admitted. "He likes to remind me and Edon about how he feels about you. He's told both of us that he's in love with you. But did you ever stop to consider that he's walked away from you because he loves you? Maybe he's trying to keep you safe, and this is the only way that he knows how to do that."

"Well, that's just not acceptable," Rovena insisted. "I'm his wife and the mother of his child. He owes me more than that. He can't just walk away from us. If I tell him about the baby, he won't leave me again. He wouldn't do that."

"Have you told anyone else about the baby? If the Tirana family finds out that you're pregnant, it might not end well for any of us," Bek reminded.

"I didn't plan on telling anyone before telling Jak. He

deserves to be the first to know—well, fourth, counting you, me, and my doctor," she said.

"You were staying at my house and you're pregnant with a Tirana baby. That puts us all in danger," he said.

"You have a Tirana baby in your home already. No one knows about mine yet, so I'm pretty sure that you're safe," she insisted.

"It's not the same and you know it," Bekim shouted. "If you tell Jak about the baby, he might share the news with his family and then, we're all screwed."

"Would you have turned me away had I not told you about the baby?" Rovena asked. She already knew his answer. There would be no way that Bekim would ever turn her away, for any reason.

"No," he breathed. "I'd have your back, sis, always."

"I know that Bek and it's why I came to you as soon as I found out about the baby. I was worried that I wouldn't be able to keep both of us safe at my cabin. If the Tirana's are still coming for me, that will be the first place they'll look."

"Well, if they come looking for you at my place, I'll keep you safe, but you're right—this is something that Jak should know about. He should know what he's giving up if he decides to stay away from you. Just be careful, sis." She wasn't sure what she'd do if he didn't agree to come home with her, but one thing was for sure, she'd take care of their baby and keep him or her safe.

JAK

Jak knew that Teodor was going to double cross him before he even got to the airport. He had decided to call Edon to give him a heads-up about being found. If he wasn't going to be around to protect Rovena, he wanted to make sure that her brothers would be. That was when Edon told him of the deceit and betrayal that Jak was walking straight into.

Edon had some guys on the inside of the Tirana syndicate, and he had heard that the plan wasn't to bring Jak home to Albania and let him make amends by working for the Tirana family. No, the plan was to murder him before he could even step foot on the plane. A part of him wondered why Teo didn't just do the job at the abandoned strip mall, but Edon pointed out that would put him and the Tirana family in hot water with the American authorities. That was something that the families tried to avoid at all costs. If Teo had killed Jak at the strip mall, he'd be wanted by the American government and that wouldn't play well for his father.

Once Jak wrapped his head around what Edon was telling him, he decided that heading to the hangar was a bad idea. Instead, he and Edon were working out a plan to get Jak to a safe house, and then, Edon would work with Bekim to keep Rovena safe. That was all Jak wanted—his wife safe.

When he found out that Teo had taken off from Colorado to head back to Albania without him, he thought for sure that his troubles were over, but he was wrong. Teo called to let him know that he'd be seeing him real soon and that thought had him terrified—not for himself but for Rovena. She wouldn't have anyone to protect her, and Jak knew that he had to stay close to her. So, he settled two towns over from their cabin, laying low until he and Edon could come up with a good plan. Edon tried to convince him that telling Rovena what was going on would be a good start, but Jak disagreed. If she knew that the Tiranas were coming for them and had caught up to him, she'd demand that they stand their ground and fight, and that was the last thing that they should do. His family was too powerful for them to go up against alone. They'd need Edon's full backing and until he could get some guys on the ground in Colorado, he wouldn't have the help that he needed to keep either of them safe.

But staying away from his wife was turning into a nightmare for him. He had been tracking her every move without her knowing, and when she went into the clinic in town, to see a doctor, he nearly lost his mind with worry. Jak stormed into that office building, demanding to know what was wrong with his wife, but no one would tell him. It wasn't until he found her cupping her tummy with her hand, crying on the front porch of their cabin, talking on the phone to someone, that he knew the truth. She was pregnant with his baby and there was no way that he'd let her go now. He wanted to be with her and be there for every step of her pregnancy, but first, he'd have to make a new deal with his uncle.

Jak pulled his cell phone from his pocket and sat on the crappy mattress in the cheap hotel room that he was staying in. He hated that place and couldn't wait to get home to Rovena and the cabin that she had made into a home for them both. It was going to be where they raised their family and that meant everything to him.

"Hello," his uncle answered. Jak was using a burner phone to conceal his location, but he knew that he couldn't spend too much time on the call for fear of it being traced.

"Uncle," Jak said.

"Jak," his uncle breathed. "I thought we had a deal and that you were coming home to work for the family again."

"Yeah, I thought that we had a deal too until I found out that Teo was going to double cross me and leave me for dead at the hanger. He'd have an escape plan ready and wouldn't have to deal with the American authorities. Did I get that all right?" he asked. He could tell by the exasperated sigh on the other end that he had.

"So, it's true—we have a mole in the family then," his uncle grumbled as if that was the only problem he'd have to deal with.

"You'd be surprised about how many of the family members are on my side of this, Uncle. My father's loyalty to the family left me with a great number of allies. You'd do well to remember that the next time you try to double cross me."

"Why are you calling, Jak?" his uncle asked. "Do you just want to point out my failure to kill you, as I did your parents, or do you have a point." Hearing his uncle admit that he had killed Jak's parents wasn't a surprise. He had suspected it for a long time now, but that didn't make it feel less of a betrayal.

"I'm calling to make you another deal," Jak offered.

"I can't wait to hear it," his uncle mumbled.

"I'm sure," Jak drawled. "Leave me and Rovena Garo alone to live our lives here in America, and in return, I promise that neither of us will ever return to Albania. You won't have to worry about me challenging you for my position as head of the Tirana Syndicate."

"Your position?" his uncle challenged.

"Yes," Jak spat. "My father was the head of the Tirana family until you had him and my mother murdered. The only reason you've kept me around all these years is because I've remained silent and complacent. What would happen if all that changed?" Jak asked. He knew that he was poking the bear, but he needed his uncle to agree to this new deal. It would be the only way that he'd be able to keep Rovena and their child safe.

"You wouldn't dare," his uncle shouted. "You don't know the first thing about being the head of this family."

"No, I don't but I've been told that I'm a quick study and I think that I'd have enough family members backing me that you'd be out of your coveted position in no time. What's it going to be, Uncle?" he asked. "My and Rovena's freedom for the security of your head of household position?" Jak asked.

His uncle's silence on the other end of the call gave him hope. Jak was holding his breath, waiting for him to answer. "You have a deal," his uncle agreed. "But I do have to warn you that some of my men have reached out to Rovena, posing as you and they are meeting her now."

"If she dies, all deals are off," Jak shouted. "Tell me where the meeting is," he demanded. His uncle rattled off the address and Jak didn't bother with polite formalities. He ended the call, grabbed his keys, and started for the door. There was no way that he'd let his uncle's men get to Rovena before he did. He couldn't lose her—not now that they were so close to having everything that they wanted—namely their freedom.

ROVENA

"This doesn't feel right," Rovena breathed.

"That's because it's not. Jak didn't send you that message, his uncle's men did." Bekim nodded to the back of the parking lot to where an unmarked black van sat. "I'm betting that Jak didn't buy a new vehicle."

"Yeah, that's not his style. So, you think that this is an ambush?" she asked.

"Yep, and that means that we are out of here," Bek insisted. There was no way that she was going to run from this.

"What if they have Jak and he's in there?" she asked, nodding to the abandoned building. It looked as if the gas station hadn't been in business for years. The vegetation was overgrown, and the pumps were rusting out.

"Then, we'll figure that out later. Edon and I will come up with a plan to help Jak, but you're staying out of this," he insisted.

"There is no way that I'm going to let the father of my baby sit in there and not do something to help him," she hissed.

"And I'm not going to let you go charging into that building and get your baby and you killed. Jak would never forgive me if I did that," Bekim insisted. "I want you to stay put, do you hear me? I'll go in and check things out for myself if you promise not to move a muscle."

"You'll need backup," she said. Bek shot her look as if she had lost her mind and Rovena couldn't help but roll her eyes at her overly cocky brother. "Never mind," she breathed. "Just be careful."

"Will do," Bek agreed. "You stay put." She nodded and watched as her brother got out of the car and made his way into the front of the abandoned convenience store. She was sure that this was all a very bad idea, but her brother was right, she couldn't go running into the building and possibly put her baby in harm's way.

She just about jumped out of her skin when the driver's door opened, and Jak hopped into the car. "Jak," she breathed, "you're here."

"I am," he whispered.

"But you left," she reminded. She had so many questions running through her mind, but none of them were coming from her mouth.

"I didn't go far, honey," he said. "My cousin found us and the thought of him getting to you scared the hell out of me. I agreed to go back home with him to keep you safe. We had a deal, but Teo was planning on double-crossing me the whole time. Edon clued me in, and well, I never showed up to the hangar to get on the jet to go home. I've been about two towns over so that I could keep an eye on you."

"I know," she whispered. "Edon told me where you were, but I figured you didn't want me. I told myself that you would have come back to our cabin if you wanted to be with me."

"I wanted to be with you, honey, but I also knew that it wasn't safe. Teo promised that he'd be back, and I couldn't put you and our baby in danger." He cupped his hand over her tummy, and she gasped.

"You know about the baby?" she asked. "Did Bekim tell you?" She was going to kill her brother if he had spilled the beans about the baby. She wanted to be the one to tell Jak that he was going to be a father.

"No," he breathed. "I've been watching you. I know that you went into the clinic, and I might have acted like a madman, demanding that they give me answers as to what was wrong with you, but they refused. So, I followed you back to the cabin and watched you from afar. I saw you cup your tummy and realized what was going on. I take it that I've guessed correctly?" he asked. Rovena nodded and swiped at the hot tears that spilled down her face.

"Don't cry, honey," he begged. "I'm happy about the baby."

"But if you can't be with us, what will I do? I can't raise this baby alone," she insisted. That was one of her biggest fears—being a single parent as her father was left to be. He wasn't the best at being a dad, but he had a lot on his plate after her mother passed away. "I have no idea how to be a mom," she whispered.

"And I have no idea how to be a dad, but we'll figure it

out together," he assured. "Just give me a chance to prove to you that this can work, Rovena. I've made another deal with my uncle. That's why I'm here. He has agreed to leave us in peace if we agree to stay in America."

Rovena was startled when the van's engine, in the back of the lot, roared to life. "I think that someone should tell them that you made a new pact with your uncle," she said, nodding to the van.

"He's already called them off," Jak promised. She held her breath as the van full of Tirana men pulled past them and left the abandoned lot.

"Bekim," she shouted, suddenly remembering her brother's absence. "He's in that building."

"Shit," Jak shouted. He got out of the car and Rovena followed after him into the empty store. "Stay behind me," he ordered.

She fell in line behind him, grabbing handfuls of his shirt, and bunching it into her fist. Rovena worried that Jak's uncle's men didn't get the message to call things off before finding her brother in the building. She spotted Bek lying in the back corner of the room and gasped.

"He's over there," she shouted, pointing to her brother's lifeless body. They made their way over to Bek and Jak rolled him over. Her brother's groan filled the empty room, and she breathed a sigh of relief. "He's alive."

"Yeah, you're still stuck with me, sis," Bek grumbled. "But I think that I might have a concussion and my wife is going to kick my ass for getting myself mixed up in this mess. I promised her to stay out of things. We are not telling her that I came into this building alone knowing that the Tiranas were in here."

"Got it," Jak agreed.

"You're here," Bek said as if suddenly realizing Jak's presence.

"I am, and I'm not going anywhere again," Jak promised pulling Rovena into his side. "I've made a deal with my uncle, and he's agreed to leave us alone."

"What did you have to give up to get that deal?" Bek asked.

"I promised never to return to Albania and never to challenge him for the head of household position, since it's technically mine," Jak said.

"And you have the family's backing to take the seat from him," Bek finished.

"Yep," Jak said.

"I guess that's why his guys only knocked me out when they found me snooping around, trying to find you. I thought for sure that I was a goner. They had their guns pointed at me and then, bam, someone hit me in the head from the side. I guess your uncle's orders to clear out came just in time to save my life," Bek said.

"Thank God for that," Rovena breathed. "I don't know what I would have done if anything had happened to either of you."

"Well, now you won't have to find out," Jak assured. "I think it's time that we went home, honey," he said. They helped Bekim up from the floor and he moaned again. Jak put his arm around her brother and Rovena did the same.

"How about we take my brother to the hospital first, to get checked out, and then, you can take me home?" Rovena asked.

"That sounds like a plan to me," Jak agreed. "Then, we can talk about you marrying me again."

"Again?" she asked.

"I think that we should do things right this time and that your brothers should be there, don't you?" Jak asked.

"I agree with Jak," Bek said, putting in his two cents. "I'd love to be the one to give you away, sis," he said.

"I'd like that too," she agreed. "I'd love to marry you again, Jak," she said. Rovena wasn't sure how she had gotten so lucky, but she had. The boy who stole her heart, all those years ago, was now the man she was going to spend the rest of her life with. Lucky didn't even begin to cover it.

The End

What's coming up next from K.L. Ramsey? Buckle up and get ready for Legend (Royal Bastards MC: Huntsville, AL Chapter Book 11), coming in June 2023 from K.L. Ramsey!

LEGEND

"Well, if it isn't the legend in his own mind," Mayhem called as he walked into Savage Hell.

"Shut the fuck up," Myles shouted back over his shoulder. The guys loved to give him shit because of his name, and he couldn't do anything about his damn name. Anyway, he could have been stuck with a lot worse than Myles Legend. The guys around the club had taken to calling him Legend since he patched over from the Royal Bastards chapter out in California. Honestly, he missed home, but when Uncle Sam tells you that you're moving to Huntsville, Alabama, you move. He still owed the Army another three years and for now, Redstone Arsenal was going to be his home.

Myles liked his new club, for the most part. He could have done without the guys ragging on him all of the time, but he was sure that was just their way to initiate him into the fold. They were a good group of men—mostly ex-military. A few of them were still enlisted, like him. He was probably one of the youngest guys in the Huntsville chapter of the Royal Bastards, at just twenty-seven, but that didn't bother him much. He liked a challenge and trying to fit into his new club was proving to be quite a challenge.

He had trouble fitting in a lot of new places when he was a kid. He was an Army brat, his father always having to move them from one place to the next, but he had gotten used to it. Maybe that was why Myles seemed to adapt so quickly to new places now that he was living that life. When he was eighteen, after he graduated from high school, he announced to his parents that he was following in his old man's footsteps and joining the Army. His mother was less than thrilled by his announcement, but Myles could tell that his father was proud. God, the man didn't stop smiling for months after he told him the news. He served six years and then decided to re-up his contract, signing up for another six.

With only three more years to go, he was beginning to think about his next move. He didn't have it in him to re-up again. Honestly, he was ready for a change and Myles was sure that would involve something in private security back home, in California. For now, he was just trying to get settled in and find his niche in the Royal Bastards and at work on the base. So far, he was unsuccessful at both, but he wasn't a quitter. He'd just keep trying until he found where he belonged.

Myles sat up at the bar and looked around the club to

see who else was there tonight. "You look like you had a long day," Bowie said. "How are things down at the arsenal? God, sometimes I really miss that place, and sometimes, I drive by there and cringe."

"Yeah, I know how you feel," Myles said. "I know that I've only been here four months now, but I still don't feel like I've gotten my feet under me, and that's unusual for me. I usually find some way to fit into my new surroundings pretty quickly." He prided himself on fitting in fast. Hell, in most of the places he was stationed, he had a girlfriend within the first two weeks. In Alabama, he hadn't even gotten laid once—something that his dick tried to remind him of daily.

"Well, you know that Savage and I would be happy to help you acclimate in any way you need. All you have to do is ask." He was hoping that Bowie would make him an offer like that because he had a big ask, and Bowie and Savage would be just the guys to help him out.

"Honestly," Myles said, "I'd really love to meet someone," he admitted.

Bowie barked out his laugh, "Man, all you have to do is just look around. There are plenty of women around here every night."

"Um, that's great man, but I was hoping to find something more like what you and Savage have," Myles said. He figured out that he was bisexual when he was about fourteen. He dated both men and women in the past, but he really stuck to women because it was just easier. Maybe that made him a coward, but he couldn't help it. So many things in his life were up in the air, moving around all the time, he needed easy in his life.

"You mean, you're looking for a man and a woman to share your life with?" Bowie asked. He and Savage were together, along with a woman, Dallas, who was their wife. They were in a loving, committed relationship, and that was exactly what Myles wanted for himself.

"Yes," Myles said, "that's what I mean. Do you think you could help me out? I mean, is there a bar that you met Savage at or something?"

"Actually, Savage and I met at Redstone Arsenal. He was testing rockets for the government, as a civilian contractor, and I was still enlisted when we hooked up."

"Really?" Myles asked. Being the new guy, he had missed out on so much of the club's members' histories. He had a lot to catch up on. "How did the two of you meet Dallas?"

"Well, that's a little bit of a longer story. The abbreviated version is that she and Savage were involved before he met me, and she got pregnant just before he ghosted her."

"Wait, Savage ghosted Dallas after he found out that she was pregnant?" Myles asked. He liked their club's Prez, and he couldn't imagine the guy taking off on a woman after being told about her having his kid. He knew that the three of them had a ton of kids, and Savage seemed like a great father.

"No," Bowie said, "Savage had no idea that Dallas was pregnant. She kept it a secret from him because he ghosted her before she got the chance to tell him. Honestly, it took a lot for Dallas to come around and accept what Savage did to her. He was struggling with coming out and telling everyone that he was bi, but it all worked out in the end, and the three of us are very happy."

"Yeah, I can see that with my own eyes," Myles admitted.

"It gives me hope that I might find a way to live that same dream myself."

"I get it," Bowie said, "sometimes, I feel like I need someone to pinch me. It's like living a dream that I never thought was possible, but it is. You just have to have an open mind and try to find the right man and woman to be a part of your dream."

"I've tried to be patient and wait for them, but I think that it's not working. Maybe I should just try to find someone to date and see where that goes because looking for a threesome has been impossible to find."

"I'm sorry that I couldn't be of more help," Bowie said.

"No, it's fine," Myles said. He would have his work cut out for him, but Bowie was right—it would be worth the wait if he ever found what he was searching for. It just seemed damn near impossible to find two people who wanted what he did.

"You'll get there, man," Bowie promised. "For now, there's a woman in the back of the bar who's been stalking you since you got in. Maybe you should take her this and strike up a conversation. It couldn't hurt." Bowie held out a bottle of beer to him and Myles looked back at the woman he was talking about.

"No, it couldn't hurt," Myles agreed. "Thanks for the help, man," he said, taking the beer from Bowie. He grabbed his own beer from the bar and walked to the back of the room to find the sexy little blond who smiled up at him when he got to her table.

"You alone?" he asked.

"I am," she said, "is that for me?" she asked, nodding to the beer he held for her.

"If you'd like," he said.

"Well, then, you should sit down," she said, nodding to the seat next to her. Bowie was right—he needed to take things one step at a time, and maybe, someday, he'd find what he was looking for.

GENESIS

Genesis Dowell had one thing and one thing only on her mind—to meet the man whom she saw every day on base. Of course, he never saw her —no one did. She was easily overlooked in her coveralls, with her hair pulled up in a tight bun. She never wore any makeup to work, and that was because as a civilian contractor, she was given strict rules to follow. Those rules never really bothered her, but they never helped her to get noticed by anyone. She blended in, and when she followed Myles Legend to the bar where he hung out, just about every evening after work, she came up with a plan to get him to finally take notice of her.

She went shopping and purchased the skimpiest dress that she could find, and a pair of heels that made her look long and lean, just like the models in the magazine. Sure, she had to figure out how to walk in them, but the shoes were worth every ounce of pain that they had given her.

She watched videos to learn how to figure out what shade she was and how to purchase the right makeup for her skin tone. She even went to a salon to get her hair cut and styled, so that when she wore it down, it wouldn't just hang around her face, making her look like a stringy little mouse. It took a lot of planning, but it all became worth it when she saw Myles walking across the bar with his eyes on her. She had finally gotten his attention and she planned on keeping his eyes on her for the whole night.

She finished about half of her beer before he finally asked her name. "My name is Genesis, but everyone calls me Gen," she told him.

"Nice to meet you, Gen, I'm Myles."

"Nice to meet you too, Myles," she said, holding her hand out to him. He shook it and smiled back at her. She hadn't planned on telling him that she worked at the Arsenal, but he looked her over, squinting his eyes at her, and she knew that he was trying to figure out where he'd seen her before.

"Have we met before?" he asked.

"No," she breathed, "but it wasn't for lack of trying. I work at the Arsenal and have seen you around," she said. "I guess that's why I was shamelessly staring at you from across the bar. Sorry about that," she lied. She wasn't sorry at all. Gen had been planning on meeting him for weeks, she just had to figure out how to do it.

"So, you've seen me around base?" he asked.

"Yes," Gen breathed.

"I guess I'm just trying to figure out how I miss seeing you," he said.

"Well, I'm a civilian contractor and I'm under orders to

wear these really gross overalls and my hair pulled back. Oh yeah, I can't wear makeup either, so I usually don't look like this." She held her hands wide for him to get a good look at her.

"Still, I'm pretty sure that I'd remember seeing you around the base," he insisted.

"I've been told that I'm really good at sliding under the radar. I mean, most people don't even know that I'm even in the same room with them. I guess I'm pretty unforgettable," she said. "Sorry, I know it sounds like I'm being a Debbie downer, but that's not what I'm going for. I'm just saying that you don't have to be upset about not noticing me because not many people do."

"Well, I'm noticing you now, Gen, if that means anything," he said. It meant everything to her that he was sitting at the table with her, having a conversation that she had never dreamed to be possible. She smiled and nodded, not knowing what to say or talk about next. She planned to do very little talking and get Myles to take her back to his place, but she'd blown that when he asked if they knew each other. Gen wasn't sure if she'd be able to recover from her admission, but she had to try.

"You seem a little nervous," he said, "are you all right?" Gen looked down to where her hands trembled on her beer bottle and pulled them down to her lap.

"Oh, yeah," she said, "I get nervous when I meet new people, but I'm good," she promised. She was anything but good. She was screwing this all up and she was worried that she'd never get another chance at this if Myles walked away from her. She really wanted her chance with him.

"I'm sorry," she said, "I just really wanted to meet you

and I'm afraid that I'm screwing this all up." She stood and he grabbed her hand into his own.

"How about you stay and have another drink with me, Gen?" he asked. "I don't think that you've screwed up anything."

"Really?" she asked. "I mean, I practically stalked you to find you here," she admitted. "Although telling you that probably isn't helping my case."

He chuckled and shook his head, "Not really, but I'm flattered. Please, have another beer with me," he insisted. Gen sat back down in her chair, and he thanked her—actually thanked her for staying.

He waved to the guy at the bar who nodded back at Myles and brought them each another beer. She wasn't much of a drinker, and Gen knew that two beers were usually her limit.

"These are from the guy sitting at the bar, in the corner," the bartender said. Myles looked across the bar at the guy and cursed under his breath.

"Thanks, Bowie," he said to the bartender.

"Do you know that guy?" Gen asked.

"I do," Myles admitted, "we work together, and I thought that he hated me. Why would he send us over a round?"

"Um, I'm not sure, but it looks like you're going to be able to ask him yourself in just a few seconds," Gen said, nodding to the guy as he made his way through the crowd to where the two of them sat.

"Legend," the guys said. He nodded to Gen, "Ma'am," he said.

"Gavin, this is Genesis, but everyone calls her Gen. What are you doing here?" he asked.

"Good to meet you, Gen," Gavin said, taking her hand into his own and holding it for a bit too long after he got done shaking it.

"You too, Gavin," she said.

"You work on base, don't you?" Gavin said.

"Yes," she breathed.

"I was sure that I had seen you around. You're a civilian contractor, aren't you?" he asked.

"Yes," she said. That apparently was the only word she could get out.

"You never said why you're here at my club, man," Myles said.

"Well, Legend," Gavin started.

"I thought you said your name was Myles," Gen interrupted.

"It is, my last name is Legend, and we usually go by last names, right Parker?" he asked.

Gavin shrugged, "Sure," he agreed, "and to answer your question, I kind of followed you here, and well, here we all are. I didn't know that you two are dating."

"We're not," Myles said. He was so quick to tell his buddy that they weren't on a date, which kind of hurt Gen's feelings. But technically, they weren't on a date, even though she was nervous enough to feel as though she was.

"I see," Gavin said, pulling out a chair to sit next to Gen.

"Sure, have a seat, man," Myles drawled.

"Um, if you two will excuse me, I need to run to the ladies' room." Gen stood and grabbed her purse.

"Hurry back," Gavin shouted over his shoulder as she left the table. She didn't look back at the two guys she had just left behind, because if she did, she wouldn't just go to the bathroom, but high tail it out of that bar and never go back again. Honestly, that might be a better choice, but she was still hoping to get some time with Myles after he and his friend got done talking. The question was, would he want to spend some time getting to know her after she acted like a nervous wreck around him?

GAVIN

Gavin Parker wanted to talk to the pretty beach bum that had shown up on base a few months ago. God, Myles Legend was just his type, but he couldn't just blurt that out around the base. No, if he wanted his chance with Legend, he'd have to find him on his own turf and talk to him privately.

"So, you followed me here?" Legend asked.

"Yeah, I hope that was okay. Honestly, I just wanted to talk to you, and I didn't want to do it around the Arsenal."

"That seems to be the running theme here tonight," he said.

"What?" Gavin asked.

"What I mean is that you're not the first person to follow me here tonight," Legend said.

"Do you mean Gen?" Gavin asked. "She followed you here too?"

"Yeah, and I'm trying to figure this all out. I mean, she

said that I didn't notice her on base, so she kind of stalked me to see where I went after work every day, and now, you're telling me the same story. I'm just trying to keep up here," Legend said.

"How about you don't try to figure it all out and just go with it?" Gavin asked.

"You haven't known me very long, Parker, but that's just not my style," Legend admitted.

"Well, we have been working together for the past few months, and I see you just about every day," Gavin said.

"Right, and don't forget that you follow me around after work," he said.

"Yeah, there's that too," Gavin teased. "I'm not trying to freak you out, but I just wanted a chance to talk to you outside of work," he said.

"Okay, what would you like to talk about?" Legend asked. He wasn't sure if just blurting it out was a good idea or not. Gavin had never been one to put himself out there when it came to dating—especially when it came to dating men. He hated feeling so unsure of himself, but when it came to asking a guy out, he was a nervous wreck. It was so much easier to ask a woman out. Hell, he didn't even know if Legend liked guys. Gavin had thought that he had picked up on those vibes coming from Legend but walking into Savage Hell and finding him sitting with a woman in the corner of the bar had him rethinking his whole plan.

"I'd like to talk about the possibility of you letting me take you out on a date," Gavin said. God, why was it so hard to choke out those words?

"You want to go on a date with me?" Legend asked.

"I do," Gavin admitted.

"Shit," Gen said, standing over their table. Apparently, she had come back from the ladies' room, and he hadn't even noticed. "I was going to ask you out on a date," she said to Legend. "But it seems that Gavin beat me to the punch."

"Gen," Legend said.

"No, it's fine," she insisted, "I hope you two will be very happy. I'm going to go home now." She took one last sip of her beer and started for the front door.

"I'm sorry, man," Gavin said. "I didn't mean to butt in here. I didn't know that she was going to ask you out. Hell, I thought that you were gay, but no biggie," he said. He felt like an ass, and he decided that Gen had the right idea about running out of that bar as fast as humanly possible.

"I've got to go," Gavin said, standing. He quickly paid his bar tab on the way out and didn't bother to look back at Legend. He didn't have the nerve to face down something that he wanted so badly but would never have.

He was almost to his bike when Legend shouted for him and Gen to stop. He looked across the parking lot to where Gen was fumbling through her purse and if he wasn't mistaken, she was crying.

"Can you both come back over here, please?" Legend asked. He wasn't really asking either of them, more like giving an order, and that turned Gavin completely inside out with need. Gavin put his helmet back on his bike and followed Gen back over to where Legend stood.

"What do you need, Myles?" she asked. Gavin saw the tears that streamed down her cheeks and God, she was breaking his heart. She really liked Legend.

"I want to go out with you on a date, Gen," Legend

admitted. Hearing him say that to her felt like a slap in the face to Gavin.

"Gee, thanks for calling me back over here to listen to you tell Gen that you want to accept her date offer," Gavin spat. "This has been great."

He turned to leave, and Legend shouted after him. "I want to go out with you too, Parker," he said.

"Wait, how can you accept both of our date offers?" Gen asked.

"Because he's bi, aren't you?" Gavin asked.

"I am," Legend admitted, "I like to date men and women, and I'm hoping that you feel the same way, Parker," he said. Gavin was starting to figure out where Legend was heading with all of this.

"I do like to date men and women," Gavin agreed. "Gen, would you like to go out with me?" he asked.

"I'm so confused," Gen breathed. "I can't go out with both of you."

"Sure you can," Legend insisted. "We can go out together—all three of us."

"How will that even work?" Gen asked. Gavin wasn't sure if they were going to have to paint her a picture or just explain the basics to her. Either way, this was going to be fun.

"Are you attracted to Legend?" Gavin asked.

"Yes," she breathed, smiling over at him.

"And are you attracted to Parker?" Legend asked.

"I mean, we just met, but yes—he's handsome," she admitted. Gavin puffed his chest out a bit, making them both laugh.

"Great," Legend said, "I'm attracted to both of you."

"Same," Gavin quickly added, "so, we can all go out and see where this ends up. Are you up for that, Gen?" he asked.

"I have no idea," she said, "but, I want to tell you that I am."

"So then, say that," Legend insisted.

She looked between them, seeming so unsure of what her answer should be. "All right," she finally breathed. "I'll go out with both of you, at the same time."

"That a girl," Gavin said. He was finally going to have a chance with the sexy guy he worked with over the past few months and now, he had the added bonus of having Gem along too. Following Legend into that bar was the best idea that he had had in a long time, and now, he had a date that he was finally looking forward to.

Legend (Royal Bastards MC: Huntsville, AL Chapter Book 11) Universal Link->
https://books2read.com/u/mBVrKM

Do you love Mafia Romance? Then you won't want to miss the book that started it all! Llir: Tirana Brothers Syndicate Book 1 is available now!

ELIRA

TIRANA

BROTHERS TRILOGY

"Get in the fucking car or I will put you in the trunk," he spat. She sneered at him knowing that it would earn her a backhand to the face again, but she didn't care anymore. There was no way that she wanted to get back into his car knowing that it might be the last time she got back out. Every time he moved her; she was sure it would be the last. She was waiting for him to find a reason to kill her and just be done with this ugly game he was playing, but the end never came. Hell, maybe she was hoping for him to finish her off—end her life and let her go, one way or the other.

"No," she whispered. Her voice was so soft she wasn't even sure that she had spoken.

"What the fuck did you just say?" he asked.

"No," she said a little louder and bolder. If this was the end, she'd find a way to muster enough strength to face it with dignity.

"Kuçkë e ndyrë," he shouted. Calling her a fucking cunt would have usually hurt her feelings, but honestly, she didn't care what he thought of her. He was so close; she could feel the spray of his spit as he shouted at her. His breath smelled like stale beer and cigarettes, making her want to vomit. She gagged and even dry heaved before he pulled his hand back and let his fist fly, full force at her face. Elira staggered back as far as her restraints would allow. He had a collar around her neck as if she were his pet chihuahua, and she was tethered to a leather leash he kept a tight hold on. He gave it a quick yank back and she was once again standing face to face with the disgusting pig. He stared her down and she laughed, wiping at the blood that dripped from her bottom lip.

"You know," he spat, "I thought we might be able to do this the easy way, but I guess I was wrong, you stupid bitch," he shouted. "I gave you the option to live and you threw it away." This is it—she was finally going to have her way out of the hell she'd been in for the past few months. How many days she had been his captive, Elira didn't know. She had lost count so long ago as the days and nights blurred together. It had to have been months though, even if her captivity felt like it lasted years.

"You want to die, don't you?" he shouted. "You want to be free of me but where would the fun in that be?"

Elira didn't answer him, just stared him down as if daring him to fire the gun he was holding in her face. He was right, but she'd never tell him that. He didn't know her—to him she was just a number, another woman on the auction block, another nameless face that would make his boss money. That was fine with her because she felt the same way about him—she didn't know him, nor did she want to. All the asshole in front of her was good for was one thing—pulling the fucking trigger to end her misery. But she wouldn't ask him for that—no, she wouldn't beg. "Please," would not be her final fucking words.

He shoved the barrel of the gun into her cheek, and she defiantly pushed back against its weight. His laugh was mean, and she knew he was going to do it. He didn't seem like the type of guy who liked being taunted. He'd never let her get away with that. She closed her eyes and waited for him to do it—pull the trigger. It was her mantra playing through her mind in almost a singsong voice. She wanted it, but she'd never give him the words. Elira could feel the gun press into her face just a little more and then he pulled the trigger, the "click" of the empty chamber played through the air and she held her breath waiting—for the pain, the blood, the darkness, the end. But it never came.

"Guess it's your lucky day," he spat. "You're going to auction, and you should start praying now that whoever buys your disobedient ass is as kind as I've been with you." He popped the trunk that she was backed up against and it bumped into her ass, jetting her forward, pressing her up against his sweaty, dirty body. She could feel the bile rise in her throat and if it came up this time, she wouldn't stop it. The last time he took her body against her will, she suppressed the urge to vomit, but this time she wouldn't. If he dared to touch her body again, she wouldn't hold back anything.

They had kept her in a dirty cage with about thirty other young women. The men who guarded them rotated them out. When each woman was brought back they were bloody, used, and all had the same look in their eyes—they wanted death to find them. It was all they were living for now, and the end could not come soon enough for Elira. She had been used, broken, and had her spirit beaten out of her. When they first took her, she still had some fight that made her hope for rescue. Hell, she dreamed of finding her way out of there and never looking back, but that was before they "broke her in" as the guards liked to say. When they found her, she was so innocent, so naive and trusting, but that girl was gone. In her place was a ghost—a spirit looking for refuge, and Elira was sure she'd find it at the end of a barrel.

He backed her up against the open trunk again and this time, when her knees buckled, he used that as leverage to shove her in. Elira didn't fight. What was the use? They were down by the docks and no one would see or hear her. No one was coming to her rescue. This was her life now, and her only hope was that whoever purchased her showed her no mercy. This time, when the person on the other end of the gun pulled the trigger, she wanted the darkness—she craved it.

LLIR

Llir Tirana walked into the club through the back door. He hated these fucking things, but as the acting head of the Tirana family, what choice did he have but to attend the auction? He always found these auctions to be barbaric—the idea of having to purchase a woman was foreign to him, but in Albania, it was a way of life. The Albanian human trafficking black market was what funded his family, and as one of the most influential families in the syndicate, he had no choice but to show the hell up and pretend to enjoy the show. It wasn't that bad, really—hot, half-naked women parading around on stage. Yeah—that wasn't such a bad way to spend a night. Most of the time, these events were over within an hour, depending on how many women they had to auction off. After it was over, he could find a willing woman to spend the night in his bed. No, he didn't have to pay for his pussy—he was a Tirana.

"You finally made it in," his brother, Veton said. As the youngest, he was the biggest smartass out of the three of them due to their grandmother constantly reminding Vet how special he was. Sure, their grandmother loved them all, but Veton was her baby and obvious favorite. They lost their mom when they were so young, their grandmother was like their surrogate mother growing up.

"Yeah," Llir said. "Before you give me shit, I just got back from America and dealing with that shit storm. I'm thinking we need to diversify if things don't get better with our dealings over there." They had both grown up in Albania, taking trips to America with their father. Their middle brother, Altin, had moved to America to live and came home for holidays and to visit their parents, as any good son was expected to do. But a part of Llir didn't understand his brother's desire to live in that country full-time. He liked visiting the States, but he was always happy to be back on his home soil.

Veton rolled his eyes, "They always have something holding up production over there—it's their government. They can't seem to make decisions to save their lives."

Besides being in the human trafficking game, the Tiranas were known for running guns. It was part of the family business he loved, and if he could make enough money from it, that would be all he'd do. "Keep your fucking voice down," Llir hissed. "You don't know who's listening when we come to these things."

Veton's smile was easy. "Sorry, big brother," he said. "I'll try to remember my place."

"You have a lot to learn still, Veton." His brother had one more year at university over in America and Llir knew that if his brother had his way, he'd never go back to finish. All Vet seemed to do in America was find trouble. Altin was constantly calling home to tell their father about how he had to bail Veton's ass out of jail again or pay off some police officer to look the other way. His younger brother needed to get his shit together because sooner or later, their father was going to get sick of his shenanigans and cut him off. That, of course, all hinged on whether their father got better and was well enough to come back as the head of the Tirana family. The thought of the leader of their family, their patriarch, their father, not coming back from his illness made him sad, both for his dad and for himself. Llir wasn't ready to take over full ownership of the Tirana Syndicate. Hell, he was only twenty-seven years old and the thought of taking over anything made him want to run as far and fast as he could get from every responsibility waiting for him. But what good would that do him or his family? No. As the oldest Tirana brother, he'd have no choice but to assume his role as head of the family if his father should lose his battle with cancer that was eating away at his body.

The lights dimmed and his brother seemed almost giddy. "They are about to begin," Veton said, smiling his goofy lopsided grin from ear to ear. Llir shook his head at him and sat down at the closest table to the stage. He needed to at least pretend that he was interested in all of this, and his father would have insisted that they sit front and center, had he been there with them today. They had a full house tonight, and that was good for business—at least there was that. All he wanted to do was get the hell out of that old warehouse they had turned into a nightclub. Men came for the women they were auctioning off, but then they always stayed for the booze being served. It was quite the racket that his father had come up with, and Llir was there to protect his legacy.

The first woman was pushed out onto the stage and the men cheered around him. Smoke from their cigars filled the stale air and the stench made him want to choke. He always felt like he was suffocating when he had to do this kind of shit—and he was willing to bet it had nothing to do with the damn smoke. The woman was blond and the guys didn't make him guess if she was a natural blond or not. Tonight, they had forgone putting clothes on the woman and he made a mental note to knock some heads together when this shit show was all over. If the men in the audience got to see exactly what they were buying, it took away the air of mystery that usually drove up the bidding and got them top dollar for their women.

"I like the wardrobe changes," Veton sneered. God, his younger brother was practically drooling over the hot little blond number on stage.

"You would," Llir accused. "But remember, little brother, we aren't here to bid. We're Tirana's and we don't pay for our women." Veton grumbled something about life not being fair and turned his attention back to the stage. They watched endless women being paraded around up there, most wearing little to no clothing and being led around by their guards on leashes with leather collars binding their pretty little necks. Llir had to admit, he saw the appeal of a woman wearing a collar—giving over her submission to the dominance he craved.

He lost track of how many women they had auctioned

off and was beginning to wonder if the night would ever end when the announcement was made that they were down to their last girl and she was "special". The announcer made them all sound special. Hell, they weren't in the market of selling off mundane women. Who'd pay for that?

A woman with long dark hair that fell down her waist was pushed out onto the stage and Llir sat on the edge of his seat, as most of the men in the club did. It felt as though everything slowed around him and the room suddenly got very quiet. Even the men who were sitting at the bar, starting the after-party early, seemed to stop and take notice of the fair-skinned beauty on stage. Her full, pouty lips were naturally rosy and God, she was his walking wet dream. All he could think about was those sweet lips wrapped around his cock.

She looked down at the stage and when her handler ordered her to look at the men, she stubbornly refused, even giving a little shake of her head. Llir looked her up and down, noting that her full breasts would nicely fill his hands, and the little moan that escaped his parted lips had his brother turning to look at him, Vet's lopsided smirk back in place.

"You want her, don't you?" Veton whispered. Llir held up his hand as if signaling for his brother to hush. "You do," his brother affirmed without Llir giving his answer. Veton was right—he wanted the sexy little brunette and the idea of any other man laying one finger on her made him want to tear the place down. He wouldn't allow it.

Her handler tugged on her leash, pulling her back to him, making her gag some from his efforts. The soft sob that escaped her chest nearly gutted him. He couldn't watch her being mistreated any longer and before the auctioneer could even get out a word, Llir stood and jumped up onto the stage. He walked over to her handler and held out his hand for her leash. The woman didn't look up at him, keeping her eyes trained on the stage floor below.

"Give her to me," he demanded. The handler seemed to balk at the idea of just handing her over. Llir knew the score—he might be the head of the Tirana family, but each handler got paid a hefty sum for the women they delivered. The guy he ordered to hand over her leash was one of his top men. He was one of the only handlers to bring in women every week to auction and he never gave the Tirana family any shit about his cut like some of the other guys had.

"What about my payment?" the guy spat. "She's special," he insisted. "Broke her in myself." His smile was mean and Llir knew exactly what the asshole meant by that.

"I will make sure that you are well compensated," Llir agreed. Her handler hesitated and then handed him the black leather leash that had his pretty little prize tethered to the other end. Llir handed the man a wad of cash, causing him to smile.

"Nice doing business with you, Mr. Tirana. Good luck with that one—you'll need it," her handler said. He walked off the back of the stage and disappeared into the night and Llir wondered just what he meant.

He was suddenly very aware of all eyes still being on him and his new purchase. "Let's go, Baby Girl," he said, tugging at her leash to get her to follow him off the stage. Her eyes flew up to meet his, reminding him of a violent sea during a storm—so much sadness and heartache. He could almost feel everything she had been through himself.

"Please, just kill me," she begged, a single tear running down her cheek.

"Now, why would I do that?" he asked, thumbing it away. "We haven't even started to have fun yet."

Llir: Tirana Brothers Syndicate Book 1 Universal Link-> https://books2read.com/u/mVg1wr

You can also pick up the entire 3 book Tirana Brothers Syndicate Box Set here: Universal Link-> https://books2read.com/u/mV0jDA

ABOUT K.L. RAMSEY & BE KELLY

Romance Rebel fighting for
Happily Ever After!

K. L. Ramsey currently resides in West Virginia (Go Mountaineers!). In her spare time, she likes to read romance novels, go to WVU football games and attend book club (aka-drink wine) with girlfriends. K. L. enjoys writing Contemporary Romance, Erotic Romance, and Sexy Ménage! She loves to write strong, capable women and bossy, hot as hell alphas, who fall ass over tea kettle for them. And of course, her stories always have a happy ending. But wait—there's more!

Somewhere along the writing path, K.L. developed a love of ALL things paranormal (but has a special affinity for shifters <YUM!!>)!! She decided to take a chance and create another persona- BE Kelly- to bring you all of her yummy shifters, seers, and everything paranormal (plus a hefty dash of MC!).

K. L. RAMSEY'S SOCIAL MEDIA

Ramsey's Rebels - K.L. Ramsey's Readers Group
https://www.facebook.com/groups/ramseysrebels

KL Ramsey & BE Kelly's ARC Team
https://www.facebook.com/groups/klramseyandbekellyarcteam

KL Ramsey and BE Kelly's Newsletter
https://mailchi.mp/4e73ed1b04b9/authorklramsey/

KL Ramsey and BE Kelly's Website
https://www.klramsey.com

facebook.com/kl.ramsey.58
instagram.com/itsprivate2
bookbub.com/profile/k-l-ramsey
twitter.com/KLRamsey5
amazon.com/K.L.-Ramsey/e/B0799P6JGJ

BE KELLY'S SOCIAL MEDIA

BE Kelly's Reader's group
https://www.facebook.com/
groups/kellsangelsreadersgroup/

facebook.com/be.kelly.564
instagram.com/bekellyparanormalromanceauthor
twitter.com/BEKelly9
bookbub.com/profile/be-kelly
amazon.com/BE-Kelly/e/B081LLD38M

WORKS BY K. L. RAMSEY

The Relinquished Series Box Set

Love Times Infinity

Love's Patient Journey

Love's Design

Love's Promise

Harvest Ridge Series Box Set

Worth the Wait

The Christmas Wedding

Line of Fire

Torn Devotion

Fighting for Justice

Last First Kiss Series Box Set

Theirs to Keep

Theirs to Love

Theirs to Have

Theirs to Take

Second Chance Summer Series

True North

The Wrong Mister Right

Ties That Bind Series

Saving Valentine

Blurred Lines

Dirty Little Secrets

Ties That Bind Box Set

Taken Series

Double Bossed

Double Crossed

Double The Mistletoe

Double Down

Owned

His Secret Submissive

His Reluctant Submissive

His Cougar Submissive

His Nerdy Submissive

His Stubborn Submissive

Alphas in Uniform

Hellfire

Royal Bastards MC

Savage Heat

Whiskey Tango

Can't Fix Cupid

Ratchet's Revenge

Patched for Christmas

Love at First Fight

Dizzy's Desire

Possessing Demon

Mistletoe and Mayhem

Legend

Savage Hell MC Series

Roadkill

REPOssession

Dirty Ryder

Hart's Desire

Axel's Grind

Razor's Edge

Trista's Truth

Thorne's Rose

Lone Star Rangers

Don't Mess With Texas

Sweet Adeline

Dash of Regret

Austin's Starlet

Ranger's Revenge

Heart of Stone

Smokey Bandits MC Series

Aces Wild

Queen of Hearts

Full House

King of Clubs

Joker's Wild

Betting on Blaze

Tirana Brothers (Social Rejects Syndicate

Llir

Altin

Veton

Dirty Desire Series

Torrid

Clean Sweep

No Limits

Mountain Men Mercenary Series

Eagle Eye

Hacker

Widowmaker

Deadly Sins Syndicate (Mafia Series)

Pride

Envy

Greed

Lust

Wrath

Sloth

Gluttony

Forgiven Series

Confession of a Sinner

Confessions of a Saint

Confessions of a Rebel

Chasing Serendipity Series

Kismet

Sealed With a Kiss Series

Kissable

Never Been Kissed

Garo Syndicate Trilogy

Edon

Bekim

Rovena

Billionaire Boys Club

His Naughty Assistant

His Virgin Assistant

His Nerdy Assistant

His Curvy Assistant

His Bossy Assistant

His Rebellious Assistant

Grumpy Mountain Men Series

Grizz

Jed

Axel

A Grumpy Mountain Man for Xmas

The Bridezilla Series

Happily Ever After- Almost

Picture Perfect

Haunted Honeymoon for One

Rope 'Em and Ride 'Em Series

Saddle Up

A Cowboy for Christmas

WORKS BY BE KELLY (K.L.'S ALTER EGO...)

Reckoning MC Seer Series

Reaper

Tank

Raven

Reckoning MC Series Box Set

Perdition MC Shifter Series

Ringer

Rios

Trace

Perdition 3 Book Box Set

Silver Wolf Shifter Series

Daddy Wolf's Little Seer

Daddy Wolf's Little Captive

Daddy Wolf's Little Star

Rogue Enforcers

Juno

Blaze

Elite Enforcers

A Very Rogue Christmas Novella

One Rogue Turn

Graystone Academy Series

Eden's Playground

Violet's Surrender

Holly's Hope (A Christmas Novella)

Renegades Shifter Series

Pandora's Promise

Kinsley's Pact

Leader of the Pack Series

Wren's Pack